All-Season Edie

All-Season Edie

Annabel Lyon

ORCA BOOK PUBLISHERS

Library and Archives Canada Cataloguing in Publication

Lyon, Annabel, 1971-
All-season Edie / written by Annabel Lyon.

ISBN 978-1-55143-713-2

I. Title.
PS8573.Y62A45 2008   jC813'.6   C2007-907447-2

First published in the United States, 2008

Library of Congress Control Number: 2007942831

Summary: Edie copes with family tragedy and her "perfect" sister during one tumultuous year.

Orca Book Publishers gratefully acknowledges the support for its publishing programs provided by the following agencies: the Government of Canada through the Book Publishing Industry Development Program and the Canada Council for the Arts, and the Province of British Columbia through the BC Arts Council and the Book Publishing Tax Credit.

Cover and text design by Teresa Bubela
Cover artwork, lettering and interior illustrations by Alanna Cavanaugh
Author photo by Bryant Ibbetson

ORCA BOOK PUBLISHERS
PO Box 5626, STN. B
VICTORIA, BC CANADA
V8R 6S4

ORCA BOOK PUBLISHERS
PO Box 468
CUSTER, WA USA
98240-0468

www.orcabook.com
Printed and bound in Canada.

11 10 09 08 • 4 3 2 1

KGW

for Sophie and Caleb

Acknowledgments

Thanks to everyone at Orca and especially my wonderful editor, Sarah Harvey. Thanks to my family for giving me such a great childhood to draw from.

Thanks to Bryant, always.

Contents

Fishing with the Fat Boy

A warm car makes a good place to sleep, even when you have to share the back seat with sleeping bags and the big orange cooler, and the kettle is on your lap, and they still make you wear your seat belt. I listen to the raindrops hit the station wagon, landing heavily, like magnets dragged from the gray sky to the metal roof. I watch the water slurp down the windows and listen to the *skreeking* of the windshield wipers. I'm lulled by the rhythm, and I wonder why Mom and Dad find it irritating.

"I TOLD you to get replacements," Dad says to Mom.

"You did not TELL me," Mom says to Dad. "Do not raise your voice at me." I roll my eyes and squint and press my lips together the way Mom does when she's angry.

That makes my face feel like a raisin. "EDIE," Mom shouts into the back seat, and I flinch guiltily even though she can't have seen me pull the raisin face. "Are you all right back there?" I don't answer. I close my eyes quickly and wonder if I should fake a snore. Probably too obvious. "She's asleep," Mom says to Dad. Ha. Fooled you.

I wait for them to start talking about me, but they start talking about Dexter instead. I'm peeved. Dexter is my sister and the number two most common topic of conversation in my house at the moment. She's thirteen—two years older than me—and for the first time she isn't with us on summer vacation. Instead, she's staying for two weeks with her best friend, Mean Megan. Mean Megan has long black hair and a swimming pool in her backyard, but she doesn't have a cat. She can't sleep over at our house because she's allergic to my cat—ha. Dex has been asking to stay at Mean Megan's house every year for as long as I can remember, but this year our holidays overlapped with the two-week dance camp that Dex and Mean Megan have been going to every year for as long as I can remember. Dad's boss wouldn't let him change his holidays, and Dexter and Mean Megan are ballet fiends.

Two weeks without Dexter: it's a weird thing. "Do you miss your sister yet?" Dad keeps saying, like it's a big joke, but I can tell Mom and Dad are anxious—they keep talking about her, and Mom keeps looking all distracted and calling me Dex by mistake—and it's starting to infect me. I keep thinking things like, If Dexter were here now, what would she be doing? If she were listening to this conversation, how long would it take her to call me a doofus? Sometimes I hear her voice, just as if she's right next to me. "People don't smirk when they're asleep," she's saying now. "Mom and Dad are just babying you along." I can practically feel her flicking me in the temple with her fingernail. Infection is the right word. It's like a sickness that makes me act all feverish, not like myself. I'm sure in a day or so I'll settle down and enjoy not having someone pull my hair or make fun of my clothes or act all superior every two minutes.

The number one most common topic of conversation in my house at the moment is Grandpa, who had a small stroke a few days before we were due to leave. When I think about the word "stroke," I picture a big hand coming down from the sky and stroking Grandpa, as if he were a cat. But the hand didn't know its own strength, and it knocked him to the ground instead, making him bump his head, which was why he had to stay in the hospital overnight. "Grandpa is just fine," Mom and Dad said at the time, but they also almost cancelled our holidays, so I'm not sure what to believe. At first Dexter was going to stay with Grandma and Grandpa to help out, but her dance camp would have meant too much driving for Grandma, who wanted to stay home and look after supposedly-fine Grandpa. So they worked out a compromise: Dexter would stay with Mean Megan, and Grandma would look after just-fine Grandpa. Instead of going to the Grand Canyon, we would go to one of the Gulf Islands, to a cottage on a lake less than a day's ferry-and-drive away in case we had to go home quickly. "For Dexter's sake," Mom said, like I hadn't noticed Dad taking his glasses off and rubbing his forehead seventeen times an hour, worrying about his own dad. I'm eleven. I'm not a *child*.

Somehow, after all that, here we are, driving to the lake. I wonder what the chances are of passing a Dairy Queen between here and the cottage. I wonder how long it will take to get from here to the cottage. I wonder where here is. I peek out the window through sly eyelashes, so they won't guess I'm awake. Trees, mountains, rain. Trailers lumber past, followed by big logging trucks and occasionally a sleek white Winnebago with curtains and ladders and fancy yellow stripes. I decide I'm going to live in a Winnebago when I'm older. I start thinking about hot fudge sundaes and lying in bed inside a Winnebago with curtains the color of hot fudge, watching the road and the trees and the mountains melt past as it gets darker and darker. Then I really do fall asleep as we *splosh* and *skreek* and rumble toward our summer holidays.

"Wakey-wakey, Edie," Mom says.

"No," I say.

"We're here," Mom says. "Get out of the car and help carry things to the cottage."

"Where's Dad?"

"He's phoning Grandpa from the office. Look—" Mom points down the hill and through the trees "—there's the lake." The air is cool and soft and gray. I extract myself from the car, stretching, and stand beside Mom and look. We are standing in a sloping forest of pine trees; in the distance we can just barely see the lake, like a bowlful of smoke. That's when I first see the fat boy. He's going down the path from the main office past the parking lot to the jetty, and we avoid looking at each other because we're close to the same age. As quickly as he appears, he's gone.

Suddenly everything is very quiet and still, and we can even hear the water lapping at the shore with the sound of a hundred thirsty little tongues. The afternoon sky is darkening, and far away some invisible heartbroken bird is wailing and sobbing and listening to its own echoes before it grieves again. It's like we're standing in a dark misty space between rainstorms. I'll be glad when we're inside with some lights on and the smell of supper cooking on the stove, and later on a warm bed. The bird cries out again, and I shiver.

"Like, creepy," says Imaginary Dexter, standing beside me and hugging herself. "Let's go inside, quick."

"Suits me," I say. Mom asks me who I'm talking to.

The next morning I wake to the sound of birdsong. Not the mournful bird of last night; instead, these are squeaky, squirty little birds who know a sunny day when they see one. And it is a sunny day. Last night's fog has already been seared from the lake, and there are shafts of sunlight tangled in the trees, promising a bright day.

Breakfast is miserable.

"You forgot the bread," Dad tells Mom.

"So did you, I guess," Mom tells Dad, in a way that sounds funny on the surface but doesn't make anyone laugh.

"I hate flakes," I say. "Isn't there anything else? Is there a muffin? Is there chocolate? Is there cheese? Is there—"

"NO," Mom and Dad say at the same time, the raisin twins. I eat a few mouthfuls of flakes and a couple of bites of a patchy banana while Mom and Dad carefully don't talk to each other. Dexter and Mean Megan are probably having French toast and strawberries right now. I almost hope Grandpa will get worse again so our holidays will end so we can all just go home.

After breakfast, I sit with my legs hanging over the back of the itchy sofa, reading descriptions of campsites in the Canadian Automobile Association booklet and thinking of running away and living year-round in a tent and eating macaroni and cheese every possible day of my life. I'm very fond of cheese. Some days cheese is the only thing that makes life bearable. We'll have supper and everyone else will have dessert—chocolate pudding or oatmeal cookies—and I'll sit there eating cheese. Dad asks me why I eat cheese for dessert, and I answer that it helps pass the time. Dad asks me why I say that, but I don't know.

Finally Mom gets tired of seeing me lying on the sofa. She says, "There's a lake right there," her finger jabbing toward the TV and beyond to the glint of silver behind the trees, "so will you please go and get into it if you're going to lie around in your bathing suit all day? Why don't you go boating or something?"

Boating?

So I go to the office, padding across the pine needles in my spongy blue flip-flops, *flap-flap-flap*, and ask the old man for a key to a pedal boat. He gives me a key tied to an empty bleach bottle—number seventeen—and a bright red life preserver. He wants to help tie me into it, but I know how from swimming lessons. I pad off down the path through the pine trees, *flap-flap-flap*, to the jetty.

The pedal boats are yellowy orange, like cheese, with a black stripe and steering wheel and black bumpers. They're very beautiful, even though they're meant for two people. Next time I'll bring a book to put on the other seat and possibly even a sandwich. Imaginary Dexter would never come with me anyway; she'd just lie on the jetty, working on her tan. I find number seventeen. Down on the floor it's wet, and there's a daddy-long-legs stuck to one pedal. I scrape it off with my flip-flop and swiddle my foot around in the water, which is pretty warm, and scare some tadpoles. I get in with one wet foot and one dry foot, and then a voice says, "Don't forget your pee eff dee." At least that's what it sounds like.

I look around, and I see the fat boy. I hadn't seen him before because he's lying in the bottom of a rowboat tied to the jetty, below the gunwale, with a hat over his face and no oars in sight. He's the boy I saw in the parking lot right after we got here. The only other fat boy I know is Timmy Digby from school, who stole my gym bag one time and threw it into the boys' washroom. He giggled frantically until I went in to get it, and then he blocked the door with his bulk and refused to let me out. I stood there, hugging my bag, looking at the blue tiles and the smelly ceramic lavatories and the smear of sunlight on the wall opposite the high window, and Timmy turned strangely sullen, slumped against the door. You have got to be kidding me, I thought. I wouldn't fight him or beg. Eventually a teacher wandered in, and the two of us got detention.

I think about all this for a while and then I say, "What?"

He doesn't move. "Your pee eff dee," he says. "You should put it on. Otherwise you might fall into the water and sink and drown. They'd have to dredge the lake for your body, and when they found you, you'd be all swollen up and green, with seaweed in your hair and black lips and shells in your eyes. They'd have to bury you in a closed casket because no one would want to look at you, not even your parents."

I think about all this as well. "What?" I say again.

He sits up suddenly, making the boat bob around a little. He brushes the hat from his face and squints at me. His face is very red. "It's true," he says simply. "That's what happens. I read it in a book."

I say, "What's a pee eff dee?"

"Personal flotation device."

"What's that?"

"There." He points to the innocent life preserver that I left baking on the wooden jetty.

"What's a casket?"

"The box they bury you in when you're dead."

"So who's going to die?" I say. "I can swim."

"That," the fat boy says mysteriously, lying back down in the rowboat and adjusting the hat over his face, "is what they all say."

I watch him for a while. "Don't you have a key?"

"Nope."

"Where is it?"

"Up at the office."

I wait a little longer but he doesn't say anything. Then I say, more curious than generous, "Want me to go get it for you?"

"No, thank you," the hat says gravely. "I don't really feel like rowing at the moment. But thanks for the offer all the same."

None of this is at all understandable, so I lean way over and grab my life preserver or pee eff dee or whatever and drag it over my head and pull out my hair and tie the straps around my middle. I unlock the bicycle lock chaining the pedal boat to the jetty. I start churning the pedals, shoving the jetty away at the same time while managing the steering wheel with one hand. "See ya, hat-face," I call cordially. He waves, still lying down.

I zoom up to one end of the lake but there's nothing happening up there, so I start to zoom down to the other end. Pretty soon I realize the lake is bigger than I thought, so I stop pedaling for a while and just float. That's pretty peaceful, and I wish I had brought a book. I stare down into the water, which must be very deep because I can't see the bottom. It just gets darker and darker, sort of see-through on top and velvety underneath. A creepy prickly feeling starts in the small of my back and climbs up to my neck as I think about how deep the water is, how big the lake is, how small I am, how I'm on top of all that water, and how, if I spring a leak, I won't stay on top of it all for long.

"Don't be such a drama queen," says Imaginary Dex, who it turns out came along after all. She's sitting in the other seat in her halter top and cutoffs, studying her cuticles, not even bothering to look at me. "You're wearing a life preserver, plus you can swim. If you're so scared, just go to where it's shallow. I can't believe you need me to tell you this. What are you, six?"

"What is so fascinating about your fingernails all the time, anyway?" I say.

"At least for me they're not a food group," she says. "Yours are disgusting."

"Petal Blush is disgusting," I say, naming the color of nail polish she's always touching herself up with. It's very light pink, the only color Mom will let her have. "Petal Blush. Look at me, I'm an embarrassed petal. I farted and now I'm embarrassed. You have petal fart on your fingernails."

"Jealous," Imaginary Dex says, and then she's gone. I hate it when she gets the last word.

I start pedaling again toward some wafty reeds that poke up through the water at the far end of the lake. It must be shallow where there are reeds. "I'm not afraid," I say out loud, and the sound of my own voice in the middle of the big lake where no one else can hear it is a strange thing. "La la la," I sing, listening to myself with great interest and pedaling doggedly. "Shoo-be-doo." I wonder if there are fish who can hear me. I try to think of a fish song. "What shall we do with a drunken sailor, what shall we do with a drunken sailor," I sing to the fish, "ear-lie in the morning?" It isn't exactly about fish, but it's close. I'll ask my dad if he knows any fish songs. "Way, hey, and up she rises," I sing, "ear-lie in the morning." That's a good idea, come to think of it: I decide to get up really early and take a boat out on the water and—and what? I start thinking about the fish again. Are there really fish down there? The old man at the office will know. I look into the water again and see sand and realize I'm coming up to the reeds.

They're taller than I am in the pedal boat, like a floating forest. They'd make a wonderful place to hide. I imagine hiding in the reeds at night with a flashlight and a chocolate bar or some cheese. I imagine sleeping in a sleeping bag down in the bottom of a boat in the reeds, listening to the lapping tongues of the water and the rustling tongues of the reeds murmuring to each other, hearing the sad bird who only sings at night. I look down at the pedals and think it'll have to be a rowboat, which reminds me of the boy sleeping in the rowboat tied up at the jetty. Strange.

Beyond the reeds chuckles a river that maybe can, maybe can't be navigated in a pedal boat. On the opposite shore, large trees with tangled roots overhang the water, trailing long shawls of moss. All of these things look very interesting, but just then a cloud passes over the sun, and a breeze pushes long wrinkles across the lake. It's cold and maybe it's time for lunch anyway. When I get back to the jetty, the rowboat is still there, but the fat boy is gone. I lock up the pedal boat and return the key and the life preserver to the office and forget to ask about the fish. I only remember when we sit down for lunch, which is cheese sandwiches and dill pickles and grape juice.

"Dad," I say, "are there fish in the lake?"

Dad, who has spent the morning in a deck chair under the pines reading the newspaper and drinking coffee from a green ceramic mug, looks a little dazed. "Fish?" he says, looking over the tops of his reading glasses. "Oh, I imagine." Which is a silly answer, since I can imagine them perfectly well on my own. What I want to know is whether they're really there. Hopeless.

After lunch, I decide to go for a swim. Dad gives me a long lecture about the dangers of going swimming right after a heavy meal, which I listen to impatiently. By the time he finishes, enough time has elapsed that I won't get a cramp and drown or whatever it is that's supposed to happen. "Everyone expects me to drown today," I inform Mom testily, digging through my bag for my towel. It's a nice big scratchy towel with orange and white stripes. I don't like soft cushy towels: They get the water off, but they don't make you feel dry.

I race for the door, but Mom stops me. "Edie," Mom says, and I do a squirmy little impatient dance. Mom has a blue plastic bottle in her hand. "Just stand still while I put some sunblock on you," she says. "It's dangerous to get too much sun."

"Why?" Mom pours the coconut-smelling white lotion onto her hands and rubs them together. "Cold, cold," I add, dancing up and down as Mom rubs the lotion briskly into my back.

"You could get sunburnt. You could get headaches. You could get skin cancer. Too Much Sun Is A Bad Thing." Mom makes it sound very official, like Are Those Hands Clean? and How Many Times, Young Lady? and Not Until You've Eaten Your Vegetables. "What about your sunhat?" Mom's voice pursues me down the path. Whew—got away just in time.

Down by the jetty I find a big stick, which becomes my trident since I'm Neptune, God of the Sea. I stab at the little tadpoles and scatter them. "Ha ha ha," I laugh in my deepest God of the Sea voice, until it occurs to me that I don't really want to spike a tadpole. So I throw the stick away and float on my back and spit mouthfuls of water into the air like the beluga whales at the aquarium. Then I spend the rest of the afternoon lying on my towel under the trees, reading my book as the shadows slowly lengthen, until Mom calls me in for supper.

"Come on," I say to Imaginary Dex, who's lying on a towel beside me, reading one of her teen magazines.

"Five more minutes," she says. "I'm taking a popularity quiz. So far I'm nine out of ten." I walk back up to the cabin alone.

In the evening, we walk over to the office so that Mom can phone Dexter and Dad can phone Grandpa. Dad says it's too expensive to call long-distance on the cell phone from here. I look at a rack of tourist brochures while Mom and Dad pass the phone back and forth and the lady who checked us in, who's older than Mom, prods at a Game Boy with her thumbs. "Fudge," she says every now and then.

"I know, honey," Mom is saying. "I know. I know. I know. I know." She listens for a long minute. "I know, honey," she says. "Me too." Then she says to me, "Want to talk to your sister?"

"No!" I say.

I swear I can hear Dexter's little mosquito voice, at the precise same instant, saying, "No!"

"Homesick," Mom mouths to Dad as she hangs up, making an isn't-that-cute face.

"Aw," Dad says. Then it's his turn to dial. "Mom?" he says. Mom—my Mom, not Grandma—looks over my shoulder at the brochure I'm holding. It's for houseboat rentals on a different lake. "No, it's great!" Dad says. "It reminds me of that place you used to take me when I was a kid, that fishing camp up past Hundred Mile House, you remember? Kind of sleepy and basic, but in a good way. Edie's loving it. I wanted to tell Dad about it, to see if he would remember. Oh, he is?"

Mom looks up from the brochure.

"No!" Dad says. He sounds extra-hearty, like he's disappointed and doesn't want Grandma to know. "No, we'll call later. He should sleep if he's tired. Give him our love." He hangs up.

"Grandma!" I say.

"Oh, sorry, sweetie," Dad says. He's frowning and tapping his mouth with his fingers. "You can talk next time. Do you think I should have reminded her about Dad's medications?"

This last bit is for Mom. "I think she'll have it under control," Mom says, linking her arm through Dad's. I follow them back to the cottage. Dad has his glasses off and is rubbing his forehead again. It's dark now, and the lights we left on make the cottage look almost as cosy and inviting as a houseboat. That'll be good to pretend in bed tonight: that we're in a floating house, rocking gently on deep, dark water, and if the cable breaks we might wake up far from shore and have to figure out how to get back.

The next day, I decide to do yesterday backward, which means swimming in the morning and boating in the afternoon, with lunch remaining in the middle. Not long after breakfast, I put on my bathing suit and

Annabel Lyon

take my towel down to the jetty, and here's the fat boy, dabbling at the water with his toes.

"What's your name?" the fat boy asks.

I have to think about how to answer this to avoid teasing. My full name is Edith Jasmine Snow, but the kids at school generally call me Edie-Snow-Peadie, and I don't want to tell him that. Mom calls me Edith, after my great-grandmother who died, which, let's face it, is pretty creepy and weird, and, besides, I hate the name Edith. Grandpa always calls me Albert, which is too completely perplexing for words. "How old are ya, Albert?" he'll yell at me, and I'll stand dazed, wishing he'd go yell at Dexter for a change or drop dead or something. "Edith is eleven, Grandpa," Mom will yell in his ear. "Eleven, huh?" he'll yell. "Sure is old for a dog." For a while at school they called me Torpedo after I won the underwater-holding-your-breath-swimming contest, and I kind of liked that, but pretty soon they forgot about it. Dexter calls me all kinds of things, none of which is worth repeating. All the time I stand there thinking about this, kind of balancing on one foot and chewing my thumbnail, the fat boy just looks at me. Finally I say, "Dusty." Dusty is the name of my cat.

"Are you sure?" he asks.

I give him one of my looks and he says quickly, "Hey, whatever you say. Dusty it is."

"I know your name," I say, changing the subject. "Robert. I heard them calling you."

"He's not my father," Robert responds.

I stare. He says, "My mother's my mother but he's not my father. I don't want you to think he is because he isn't."

"Oh," I say. "Want to go fishing?" I ask.

"Yes," Robert says. "But it's the wrong time of day."

"So?" I ask.

"So nothing," Robert says. "Have you ever caught a fish?"

"Of course not," I say, rolling my eyes and making the raisin face for practice. "Puh-leeeeze."

"I bet I could, if I tried," Robert says pensively. Then he corrects himself and says, "I bet we could," and I decide I quite like Robert, even though he isn't always easy to follow. All that stuff yesterday about caskets, for instance, and now this man who isn't his father. "I have a fishing rod," he says. "Only I've never used it." We look at each other and then out over the water, critically, considering. The lake is all sunlight and innocent tadpoles and happy little wavelets. But further out, hidden now but surely there—oh, surely— long silver shapes knife in and out of the reeds and slip ghostlike through the depths, unsuspecting.

"Oh, boy," I say. "Watch out, fish."

Robert goes back to his cottage and gets his fishing rod, which is bright red with a black stripe around the reel and silver earring-hoops for the line to go through. He also has a tackle box with hooks and weights and lures. There are artful little candy-colored insects, lemon and silver wasps and mint green flies and red licorice rubber worms and other confections of wings and tinsel and thread, designed to tempt the greedy fish. They'd look very nice on a Christmas tree.

After lunch, we take turns casting from the jetty for practice, which works okay once we get the hang of it, but we don't even catch a single tadpole. "The fish must be farther out," Robert says when it comes time to go in for supper. "Next time we'll take a boat out to where it's deeper." We agree to meet the next morning for a day's serious fishing.

At suppertime (tomato soup and wieners), I ask if I can get a fishing rod.

"Next year, maybe, if you're still interested," Mom says. Oh well.

From then on, Robert and I go out every day in the big rowboat and fish different parts of the lake. For a while it's quite satisfying to sit still for a long time, holding on to the end of the long taut line that slices into the water. We each bring a book and take turns slumping in the stern, reading and pulling long arcs with the rod, which feels very professional. We fish the middle of the lake; we fish in the shadow of the big trees; we fish the mouth of the little creek; we fish up the windy end of the lake with the private jetties. Nothing. I decide fish are smart.

"Something isn't right," I declare flatly. "We're doing something wrong." Robert nods glumly and sighs and reaches for the oars.

Finally we go to the office and ask the old man. He tells us to try closer to the reeds around dusk. He peers briefly at our lures, then goes into the back room and comes out with a jam jar full of dirt, which he hands to Robert. "You'll have better luck with these," he says.

"What is it?" I ask suspiciously, highly skeptical that a jar full of dirt can hold more attractions for a fish than the sparkly lures.

"Live worms," the old man says. Robert quickly puts the jar down on the counter and we thank the old man. "Just pull one out and hook it on real good," he says. "They work like a charm; the fish just gobble them up. Have fun, kids."

Robert hastily picks up his fishing rod and tackle box and the boat key and the oars and both life jackets, leaving me nothing to carry but the jam jar. "Oh, sure,"

I mutter. Will I be able to feel them squirming through the glass? What if the lid comes off and they jump all over me? Eeeewwww, I think, yuck, yuck, as I pick up the jam jar and walk very calmly down to the jetty. I place the jam jar so carefully in the bottom of the rowboat that Robert, who follows me, wide-eyed and lugging all the other equipment, doesn't even smile when I slosh my hands vigorously in the lake afterward. There, I think. Who's afraid? I'm not afraid.

We row silently out to the reeds. When we get there we spend quite a few minutes making everything shipshape. Robert can't seem to find the perfect hook, and he keeps tying and untying different ones to the rod. I have to knot my shoelaces three times each before they're comfortable.

Finally we run out of things to do. The jar is still sitting there.

"I'll open it," I say. "You can hook."

"You go first today," Robert says, hastily offering me the rod.

I shake my head. I reach down, grasp the jar firmly by the throat and twist the lid. It's stiff and comes open with a jerk, which freaks me out so much that I drop the jar. It falls on its side, spilling some dirt and one worm. There it is. Quickly we snatch our feet back. "You klutz!" Robert yells.

"I even tipped one out for you!" I retort, instantly angry. When I'm angry, I stop being scared. I set my feet flat on the bottom of the boat, right the jar and snatch the hook from Robert's hand. We glare at each other. Suddenly Robert grabs the worm and throws it overboard. Then he throws the whole jar overboard and the lid too. They sink.

"My worm!" I say, although I'm in fact enormously relieved.

Robert won't look at me. He takes up the oars. "Sue me," he says, but I have no idea what this means. All the way back to the jetty, we don't say a word to each other.

We never mention the worms again.

The next morning, I actually pay attention to my parents' conversation. A fly is droning and butting against the window (stupid—painful and stupid), which makes me look up in annoyance from my crossword puzzle. It's going badly anyway. Who's ever heard of a three-toed South American sloth, let alone knows what its official name is? Mom is fanning herself with a piece of paper the dry peachy color of car-sick pills, printed with smudgy purple ink. It's an advertisement for a local fair. Mom is telling Dad the fair is sure to have herbs and pottery and goats and local artists and baking and other interesting crafts. Very good for Edie.

Oh my god, I think.

"Oh my god," I say. "Crafts? No. Uh-uh. Absolutely not. You can count me out."

"Eee-hee-dee," Dad says, trying not to laugh. "Don't swear at your mother."

"Edith," Mom says, "you are coming with me tomorrow to the craft fair and, furthermore, you are going to enjoy yourself and that is the end of this discussion."

I cross my arms on my chest, as if to say that this fight isn't over yet. "She's just like Dexter was at her age," Dad says to Mom, and they smile at each other and then at me.

"OH MY GOD!" I shout. "How dare you compare me to that—turd?"

"That settles it," Dad says. "You're going to the craft fair tomorrow."

"Damn," I say.

"And no cheese for you tonight."

"Double damn," I say.

"Or tomorrow either," Dad says. "Are you learning these expressions from that boy you've been hanging around with? That little fat boy?"

"Robert is not FAT!" I shout. Well, he is, really, but

he's my friend, so I say, "Anyway, so what if he is?" And then, for good measure, I add nastily, "I would take being fat over going to a craft fair ANY DAY OF THE WEEK." And with that I stomp into my bedroom to change out of my bathing suit.

That evening, we make our nightly after-supper visit to the office to phone home. This time, Dad goes first.

"Dad? Dad?" he says. "Dad! How are you? No, we're fine! Are you fine? We're fine! That's great!"

Mom and I are having a thumb-war while we wait. Quietly, I say, "Why is he talking like that?"

"He's nervous," Mom says, quietly too. "It makes his voice go all funny."

"Why is he nervous?" I ask.

Mom pins my thumb.

"Okay, we were having a conversation," I say. "That doesn't count."

"Best of five," Mom says.

"Trout, I think," Dad is saying. He glances at the woman with the Game Boy, who looks up long enough to nod, looks back down and sighs. Her game makes a farting sound to show she lost. "Trout," Dad says confidently. "I sure wish you were here! You could give us pointers! Maybe next year!"

"Us?" I say to Mom. Dad hasn't come fishing once. She pins my thumb again. "Do you mind, while I'm talking?" I say. Dad hangs up. "Grandma!" I say.

"Oh, sorry, sweetie," Dad says. "Next time."

Mom phones Mean Megan's house. She starts to say something, listens for a minute and then says, "Oh, honey, I know. I know. I know."

I roll my eyes at Dad, who smiles at me vaguely. I know he isn't paying attention.

"Edie wants to talk to you," Mom says, which is a lie, but she gives me a look and holds out the phone. "Be nice to your sister," she whispers.

I take the phone. "Hex on Dex," I say.

"Greedy Edie," she replies. I hear her snuffle.

"What are you doing?" I ask.

"What are *you* doing?"

"Going to an extremely fun craft fair tomorrow." Mom gives me a look.

"What did you have for dinner?" Dex says. "We had tofurkey. Megan's family doesn't eat meat."

I tell her that's because they're from outer space, and she laughs. Then she says, "Don't make me laugh. I'm upset."

"What's that word again?"

"Tofurkey," Dexter says. "Tofurkey, tofurkey, tofurkey."

I say, "Tofurkey, tofurkey, tofurkey."

"Brat," she says. I give the phone back to Mom.

"See?" Mom says to the phone. "We miss you too."

"No we don't!" I yell so Dexter will hear.

The next morning, after breakfast, I put on shoes and socks for the first time since we arrived at the cottage. Then I bounce up and down on the itchy sofa while Mom organizes her handbag on the kitchen table.

"Where's Dad?" I ask as we walk to the parking lot. "I bet he's in the bathroom. I'll go tell him to hurry up."

"Get in the car, Edith," Mom says. "Your father's not coming. He—has a headache." She looks a little raisiny as she says this.

"Too Much Sun?" I ask. Mom presses her lips a little more, but now her mouth is twitchy. She turns the key in the ignition. Then she puts her arm on the headrest to look over her shoulder and starts backing cautiously toward the lane. "Let's hit the road," she says, and I laugh. Sometimes she says funny things like this, and then I know we'll have a good day.

We drive for about half an hour, take two wrong turns and finally arrive at a large, muddy, breezy field where the sky is sagging darkly with rain. There are tables set up with local people standing around in wind-breakers, chatting and drinking coffee from thermal cups. Mom buys a green cardboard box of blueberries. The blond lady at the table wants to give me a taste, but I can tell Mom doesn't want me to eat them until they've been washed. "Is okay," the lady keeps saying, "zese ah oh-ganically grown, yah?"

"Zese ah oh-ganic, yah?" I repeat under my breath, just for the flavor of it, but maybe not quietly enough because then Mom gives me a handful of blueberries to eat. Some are fat and too sweet and some have a sour bite, the way I like them, and afterward the palms of my hands are purple even though I lick them. Mom starts talking to the lady at the pottery table about glazing techniques, so I wander over to where some tarpaulins are spread on the ground and pretty girls in funny clothes are selling jewelry.

They say hello, and suddenly I feel shy because no one else seems to be standing over here. They have long hair and long colored skirts and sandals, and one dark-haired girl wears a silver chain with blue stones around her smooth white ankle. The blond girl who's laughing and talking has a small diamond in her nose, which is distracting. They sell complicated silver jewelry and beads and leather necklaces with crystal pendants, many of which would make good lures.

I observe all this from a cautious distance. When Mom calls me away, the strange pretty girls smile and wave. I'm vaguely aware that Mom has bought a bowl or a milk jug or something for Dexter. I keep looking back, trying to keep the diamond girl in sight. Mom tugs my hand and says, "Look, Edie, look." I turn and see something truly magnificent.

A small boy has two peacocks on leashes, like dogs. They're strutting and pecking and dragging their tail feathers on the muddy ground. They have feathers like crowns, and their throats are the world's most beautiful blue. Several of the long, rich tail feathers stand propped in an umbrella stand.

"Twenty-five cents," the boy says shyly.

When we get home, I collar Robert and bring him into the cottage to admire my find. We've been avoiding each other since the worms.

"Wow," Robert says, fingering the wispy threads of one of the feathers. "Nice."

"You want one?" I say suddenly. Robert looks at me, not sure if I'm being serious. I'm not sure if I'm being serious either, but I've said it now, and, after all, I do have three. "Go on," I say. He chooses the smallest one and picks it up gingerly between his finger and thumb, supporting its huge unwinking sapphire eye with the palm of his other hand. He looks like someone who isn't much used to holding babies. He just stands there holding the stupid thing until it gets embarrassing.

"Come on," I say. "Let's go dump it at your cottage and go fishing or something." So we do.

A couple of days later, Edie the Human Killer Whale is terrorizing the jetty when someone starts shouting.

"DUSTY!" It's Robert. He's running and puffing and shouting. I stop floating and stand up, wondering what's happened. At the jetty, he bends over and puts his hands on his knees to breathe. He's winded, and it takes a couple of seconds before he can talk. "My mom says you can come over to our cottage after supper tonight and watch a movie if your mom says it's okay."

"Yay," says Edie the Human Killer Whale, scrambling up onto the sand and jiggling furiously and squeezing her hair and shaking little sparks of water in all directions, like a dog. "I'll go ask."

Mom insists on going and talking to Robert's mom, who smokes and wears sunglasses and shorts. They stand outside under the pine trees and chat for quite a while as Robert and I fidget and squirm and make faces at each other. Robert's mom assures my mom that Robert is Very Responsible, and Mom says that's a good thing because Edie is A Bit Of A Handful Sometimes, and Robert's mom says isn't it great that the two of us Seem To Be Getting Along, and Mom says that it's so nice to see that Edie is Finally Socializing With Her Peers.

"Shut up," I say under my breath because Imaginary Dexter is leaning against a tree, laughing at me. She hasn't been around in a couple of days, but trust her to show up when things get humiliating.

"Edie has a date," Imaginary Dexter says, giggling. "With a fat boy."

"It's not a date," I say.

"Oh, I'm sorry," Imaginary Dexter says. "A *play*-date."

"Shut up!" I say. Mom and Robert's mom look at me in surprise. "Bee!" I say, swatting at my ear. "Buzzing too close! Too loud! Shut up, bee!"

"So cute," Robert's mom says and seems to mean it, but Mom gives me a narrow look that says You Will Be Explaining Yourself, Young Lady, in the Very Near Future.

Once we're back at the cottage, she gives me that eyebrows-up look that means The Future Is Now. "Sometimes I hear Dexter making fun of me," I tell her. "I hear her actual voice."

Mom's face goes soft. "Me too," she says.

"Dexter makes fun of you too?"

Mom laughs. "She tells me what she likes. She likes your peacock feathers. She liked the jewelry table at the craft fair. She can't believe you have a boyfriend. I think she's jealous."

"STOP IT!" I say. "He's not my boyfriend!"

Mom holds her hands up like she's surrendering. "I didn't say it, Dexter did!" she says, and then we both start laughing because, let's face it, one Imaginary Dexter is a pain, but two Imaginary Dexters is just weird.

After supper, I walk over to Robert's cottage and knock on the door. Robert's mom answers and calls me honey. She says Robert has just gone out for a second to get some ice, but I should come right in. She says she's just going to go put on her face. Then I'm on my own in the living room.

Robert's cottage ought to look just like my cottage, only it doesn't. For one thing, it's very messy, with clothes and magazines strewn around, and dishes from dinner that no one has bothered washing up yet. For another thing, the dark green curtains are closed so the living room looks like it's underwater. The whole place smells musty.

"Hello?" says a voice. I look up and see the man who isn't Robert's father peering out of the bedroom door. He has sunglasses and a silver bracelet and a lot of chest hair.

"What has cottage cheese got to do with cottages?" I ask. This has been bothering me all day.

There's a brief uncertain pause. "I have no idea," he says and goes back into the bedroom. Then Robert comes back with the ice, and Robert's mom comes back out looking just the way she did when she said she needed to put on her face. "We're just going to the pub up the road," she says. "If you have problems, Edie's parents are right up there." She waves her hand vaguely. I feel a little irritated that this woman is telling me where my own cottage is.

The man who isn't Robert's father comes out of the bedroom and jingles his car keys. "C'mon, hon," he says to Robert's mom.

"Well, you have a nice time, kids," Robert's mom says.

"Bye, Mom," Robert says. That's the first thing he's said since he came in.

The movie is in black and white. There are shadows and gunshots and beautiful women in hats, and men sipping drinks, but nobody bleeding or swearing at all. It's from the forties, Robert says. The men tip their hats back with their guns and sip their drinks some more and grimace.

"Bourbon," Robert informs me seriously. "Someday I'm going to try some."

"I snuck some once," I offer, my eyes still fixed on the screen. I'm wondering if the women will get to shoot anybody.

"YOU DID?" Robert shouts, making me jump. He struggles to sit up. "WOW. What was it like?" He studies me intently.

"Awful," I say. "Worse than medicine."

Robert looks incredulous. "No," he says. "That can't be right. They drink it in the movies."

"Honest," I say. "I think it's what they give you at the dentist. It hurts your tongue."

"Wow," Robert says, but thoughtfully this time. He looks disappointed. "I can't believe it. Are you sure? I bet you're fibbing. I bet you never really."

"Ask my dad," I say. "He caught me."

"Oooh," Robert says, flinching in sympathy. "Ouch."

"Yup," I say grimly, remembering. "And it wasn't even worth it, either."

"Wow," Robert says for the third time, and I see he's finally starting to believe me. "No kidding?" He squints at me, and I can tell he just thought of something else. "Do you always get caught?" he asks. "Don't you ever get away with anything?"

"No," I say. I figure getting away with something would be like catching a fish: it never really happens, not really.

After the movie is over, Robert and I walk back to my cottage. Mom and Dad are sitting in deck chairs under the pines, sipping something from juice glasses. Robert and I look at each other significantly, but I notice that Dad has his glasses off again and Mom's lips are tight, and they're not talking or looking at anything in particular until we're practically on top of them. When Dad notices us, he blinks and says, "Okay."

Robert asks, "Fishing in the morning?"

"Yup," I say.

Dad says, "Better fit it in while you have time. We're leaving the day after tomorrow."

"No we're not," I say. "We have another week."

"Change of plan," Mom says. "Grandpa's feeling just a little, little, tiny bit worse and we're going to go home early just to help out."

"Grandma phoned while you were watching your movie," Dad says.

"Tiny, tiny," Mom says because I'm looking hard at her, and she knows why.

I go to bed pondering and dream Dad is fishing from the jetty with a jam jar tied to the end of his line while the diamond girl aims a gun at him. Then he catches an immense killer whale, which drags him into the water and down to the bottom of the lake. When they drag him up again, he has black lips and there are shells in his eyes and the lake glows blindingly in the late afternoon sun with a color like laughing. It doesn't feel like a nightmare.

It seems as though my last full day at the lake will be like all the others: fishless.

"Grade six," I'm saying. "I start French immersion this year." We're talking about school. Robert lives in the city and goes to a school I have never even heard of. He has violin lessons and a pass to the planetarium. He says he can walk to the planetarium from his house and his mom can walk to Safeway, but I don't believe it. Nobody just walks to places like that.

"Grade seven," he's saying. "I like French. What I hate is gym." Then he gets a funny look on his face and tugs at the rod. "Oh no," he says.

"FISH!" I yell.

The rod jerks like a live thing. Robert starts reeling in, faster and faster. I'm practically standing up in the boat until I remember the rule and sit down with a bump. "Whack it on the head with my soda!" Robert shouts. It's hanging in the air on the end of his rod, alive.

"FISH!" I yell. Robert maneuvers it onto the floor of the boat, where it flops and heaves mightily. It's about a foot long and silver. It has eyes.

"OH MY GOD!" I yell. I grab Robert's soda can and whack the fish's head, once, to stop the awful flopping. It lies still, the hook and line still in its mouth. Robert and I are panting.

"Fish," I say.

Robert nods, speechless.

When we get to the jetty, a crowd has gathered: our parents and the old man who rents the boats, and some people from other cottages. They all heard the yelling. The old man gets the hook out of the fish's mouth (Robert and I haven't touched it yet) and weighs it by hanging it on a contraption he pulls out of his pocket and seeing how far over the needle goes. People are patting us on the back. The old man wants to gut it for us, but Mom says, "I know how."

I stare at her. "You do?"

"I grew up in Newfoundland," Mom says. "I guess I know how to gut a fish."

"You're from NEWFOUNDLAND?" I shout. I knew it, but it didn't really mean anything to me before now.

"Fish for supper," Mom says, grinning.

"Is it supposed to have this many bones?" I ask.

Mom has fried the fish in butter and breadcrumbs. It smells good, but it's impossible to eat. Dad keeps clearing his throat and glancing at Mom and eating his bread and salad. Robert, who's over for supper, is politely pulling things out of his mouth like somebody taking hairs off his tongue. I can see he's trying not to look at anybody.

However, for dessert, Robert's mom made chocolate cake. So it isn't all bad. Although a chocolate cheesecake would have been even better.

On my last morning at the lake, I sit with Robert on the jetty. I'm not even allowed to get my feet wet, and there isn't much to say. Robert asks if we'll be coming back next year. "I imagine," I say wistfully. I'm thinking about the fish. "Are you?" I ask.

"Yes," Robert says. "We're here every year." After that we watch the lake for a long time.

"EEEEEE-DIIIIIE!" Mom's voice yells.

"EEEEEE-DIIIIIE!" Dad's voice yells.

"Why are they calling you that?" Robert asks.

"Well," I explain, "it's my name."

"Oh," Robert says. "Well. See you next year, Edie."

"Bye, Robert."

"Bye."

I run up the path from the jetty through the pine trees to the parking lot, where Mom and Dad stand by our car with the old man. Some other people who have just arrived are unpacking, and everybody has about a million hands on their hips. "Young lady," Mom says, "where have you been we have been calling you for half an hour and you could at least have packed your own suitcase and you know Grandma and Grandpa are waiting and we have probably missed the ferry by now." Dad says, "No cheese for you tonight, young lady."

"Ha, ha," Imaginary Dexter says.

"Just you wait," I say. I climb into the back seat of the station wagon and whack my knee on the cooler and wedge myself down in between the sleeping bags and the electric kettle and sulk all the way home.

A Charm of Powerful Trouble

"Fat aristocrat cat sat on the brat mat," I say. I roll Dusty onto his back and make his legs do a little dance. "Dusty the Habitat Cat."

"Shut up, you troll," Dexter says.

It's Sunday afternoon. Grandma and Grandpa are coming to visit, which is why Dex and I are in the same room. Usually we manage to avoid this. Mom told us to wait together in the living room because she doesn't want to have to round us up later.

"Round 'em up, cowgirl," I tell Dusty, who yawns, showing his pink tongue and needle teeth. Bored, I consider Dexter, who's lying on the sofa, reading one of Mom's magazines. "THEY'RE HERE!" I shout, making her jump. This is hilarious. I lie on the floor, rolling and laughing, until Dexter comes over and starts hitting me on the head with her magazine. "Fight!" I yell, still laughing. My sister has a temper like a house of cards.

"Edie, leave your sister alone." Mom looks in from the kitchen, where she's making supper. "She doesn't feel well."

"I want to go lie down in my room," Dexter whines.

"All right," Mom says. I gape at this injustice, pointing speechlessly at my departing sister. "She has a tummy ache," Mom says.

"She *is* a tummy ache," I say. Outside, a familiar engine coughs and pants and chokes to silence in the driveway. "Grandma!" I say.

"See, you conjured them up with all that yelling," Mom says. I race out the front door and into the driveway. Behind me I can hear Mom calling, "Edie, socks!"

"Hello, darling," Grandma says mildly, getting out of the passenger side of their chocolate brown station wagon. Grandma is very calm and elegant and wears long sweeping clothes and clanky silver jewelry. She would never mention a thing like socks. Today she wears a crinkly black cape, like bat wings, which she uses to enfold me in a hug. Close up, she smells like oranges and spice.

"Albert," Grandpa says. He's always slower getting out of the car, even though he has a rotating cushion on the driver's seat to help him. Everybody tells me it's not a toy, but one time when I was little he sat me on it and spun me back and forth while I clapped my hands, and everyone stood around saying he was Setting a Bad Example. "Nuts!" he said. He smells like smoke and mint. It turns out he has had another small stroke, which is why we came home from vacation in such a hurry. It was a tiny, tiny stroke, as Mom said—yeah, right.

He looks just the same as usual, though, and he drove, so maybe she wasn't just treating me like a baby. After I go up to him for my hug, he fiddles around in his pocket and pulls out a nickel and gives it to me.

"What do I do with it?" I ask. I don't know anything you can buy with a nickel, not even gum, which I don't like anyway. Dumb as glue is my verdict on gum. It even makes you look dumb, chewing and chewing and never getting anywhere.

"I think it's lucky, isn't it, Grandpa?" Grandma says. She takes the nickel and blows on it. "Now, you put that in your pocket. Next time you see a fountain, you throw it in and make a wish."

"Magical powers!" Grandpa shouts, stomping up the driveway to the front door, where my family is waiting. I quickly stuff the nickel deep in my jeans pocket. "Where's Half-Pint?" Grandpa shouts. This is what he calls Dexter. "Sure is filling in, isn't she?" Dexter's face goes bright red, like she's going to cry.

Filled in, I know, means you read the newspapers every day, like Dad. Stroke or no stroke, Grandpa doesn't always make a lot of sense.

"Grandma, my stomach hurts," Dexter says in a small voice when we're all inside and Dad has taken Grandpa into the den to watch TV.

"I know, pumpkin," Grandma says. "I brought you some special tea."

I follow Dexter and Grandma and Mom to the kitchen. "Go *away*," Dexter says fretfully, but the two women soothe her. "It's all right, Dexter," they say in singsong voices, like you would use to lull a baby. They're being way too nice.

"Did you have a good time with your friend while your mom and dad and sister were on holiday?" Grandma asks Dexter.

Dexter pulls her T-shirt off her skinny shoulder to show Grandma the tan marks from her bathing suit. Where the straps were, her skin is white as a fish belly. "I caught a fish," I say, mostly to myself, remembering. The kettle shrieks. Grandma reaches into an invisible pocket and produces a small envelope, which she tips out onto the table. It contains some dried leaves and flowers. Mom scoops up the brittle sticks and leaves and crumbs, tips them into the teapot and pours the boiling water on top of them. Clouds of steam poof out of the pot, smelling like the clouds of steam that poof out of the sink when you pour in the dish detergent.

"Stinks," I say, half lying on the table, trying to see into the pot. A flower and some barky scum float on the surface of the tea-water.

"It's not for you." Grandma rearranges the folds of her mysterious clothes.

"Is it a potion?" I ask.

"It's good medicine," Grandma says.

"Dexter has her period," I singsong, and then they kick me out of the kitchen.

I go to find Grandpa in the den. He's in the recliner, sipping what looks like apple juice from one of Dad's special chunky glasses and watching golf on TV. "Look at that chip," he says, pointing at the man on the screen. He fiddles around with the side of the chair until it jerks him backward and the footrest pops up. The drink swings in the glass. We watch the little white ball fall a long, long way down and land in a lipped pool of sand. "Fudge," Grandpa says.

Mom and Dad say small strokes can give you memory loss. If I notice this, I'm not supposed to make a big deal out of it, but Grandpa just seems like Grandpa. When I tuck myself against his knee so I can rest against his chair and watch the screen over his big thick-socked feet, he reaches forward to pat my head.

He leans back again with a sigh. The golfers hike over the links, keen as explorers. I think about what it would be like if Grandpa couldn't remember me anymore.

"Here you are," Grandma says a few minutes later. "Look at the two of you. You're both almost asleep. It's time for supper. Honestly, Harvey, making poor Edie watch this nonsense. You're probably hijacking her cartoons."

"Cartoons are over," I say, quickly wiping my eyes. Grandpa still knows who I am. Crying is ridiculous.

"That," Grandpa says, pointing at the set with his thick finger. "Did you see that? Eagle."

"Bald or golden?" I say, squinting.

"Nonsense," Grandma says.

"You old witch," Grandpa says. "You're making us miss the last hole."

I giggle. Then I look up and see Grandma's face and stop. My heart starts to pound. I think, *Oh*.

At supper, I stay quiet, watching. Dexter seems happier now, eating roast and rice and peas like everyone else. Grandpa seems kind of distracted and keeps staring at his plate like he's forgotten what food is for.

"All right, Edie?" Grandma asks. "You're not eating."

Neither is Grandpa, I want to say. But before I can say anything, Grandpa sneezes. "Bless you," we all say.

But he isn't finished. He pulls a big cloth hankie out of his pants pocket just in time to catch a second, even bigger sneeze, so loud it seems to shatter the air into icy fragments, deafening us. It takes a minute to realize he's blown over his wine glass. There's a big red stain on the tablecloth, spreading by the second; shards of glass are everywhere.

"Harvey, honestly," Grandma says.

"Oh, hush up a minute," Grandpa says. "I'm covered in glass."

He is, too, bright splinters and crumbs of glass in his clothes and on the table, in our food and all over the floor. "Nobody move," Mom says.

"Jesus, Dad," Dad says. "Are you okay?"

"Don't eat any more, Albert," Grandpa says to me, ignoring him. "You might get a cut."

"You made Grandpa do that," I say to Grandma.

"Not I," Grandma says, picking a piece of glass out of her salad. There's ranch dressing on the glass.

"If that had been a mirror, you would have seven years' bad luck," Dexter tells Grandpa.

"Don't you start," Grandpa says. Mom and Dad are both up, moving gingerly around the kitchen, getting plastic bags and brooms. "I get enough of that superstitious claptrap from your grandma: black cats and lucky charms and garlic and I don't know what."

"I've been using that herb book you gave me for my birthday," Grandma says conversationally to Mom. "It's very absorbing. The history and therapeutic properties of humble garden plants—weeds, even."

"She put dandelions in my food," Grandpa says.

"Let's vacuum Grandpa," I say. I jump up and feel something go crunch. "Oh, my foot."

"Why do you think people wear socks?" Mom snaps. I know better than to point out that this doesn't make a lot of sense.

"Don't eat any more, Albert," Grandpa says to me. "You could get a cut."

"You just said that," I tell him.

"Albert could get a cut," he says to everybody else. He looks uncertain, like he doesn't know who he's supposed to say it to.

I look at Grandma. Her eyes are as bright as the piece of glass she's still holding. Dad and Mom and Dexter have gone still, like Dusty when he's trying to be invisible.

Tonight, after my bath, I go straight to bed. For once it's not because I'm in trouble, but so that I can read. I have the tiniest room in the house, with a creaking wood floor and a ceiling that slopes because it's right under the roof. Before I was born, this was the attic, but Mom and Dad fixed it up for me when I was little. There haven't been spiders up here for years, despite what Dexter says. I can handle the occasional spider anyway, if it means not having to share a room with my sister. Three of the walls are butter yellow, one with a deep-silled window where I keep my cactus and my Venus fly-trap. The fourth wall is lined floor to ceiling with shelves for my books. It's a warm, friendly place and it's all mine. If I still have a night-light, it's not because I'm scared, despite what Dexter says. It's so that if I have to use the bathroom in the night I won't trip and go down the steep, narrow, attic stairs like a basketball, *bump, bump, bump*, breaking my neck and waking everybody up.

Tonight I want a book about magic and witchcraft, but the best I can find are a couple of kiddie books about Halloween. "Throw your own Halloween party!" "Super costumes to make at home!" "Spells for kids!" That sounds interesting, but when I turn to that page I find the ingredients are things like Kool-Aid and marshmallows, which doesn't sound genuine at all. Next to the Kool-Aid spell, a cartoon of a goofy witch stirring a pot full of bubbling pink liquid reminds me of another book, one I rarely look at, that Mom and Dad gave me for my birthday.

There's a scratching at the door. Dusty's bed—a wicker basket lined with old beach towels—is down in the kitchen, but as often as not he ends up in my bed instead, which is strictly against the rules. When I open the door, he doesn't come in right away. Instead, he lowers himself into a long, luxurious curving stretch—paws down, bum in the air—and then he starts to wash. The book I want is shoved down on the bottom shelf. It's called *Shakespeare for Children*, with complicated poetry and drawings of fairies and Romans and crazy old men with beards and this one guy with a donkey's head. I skipped the poetry when I first read it; it's the pictures—one specific picture—I remember. And here it is: three hideous crones crooked over an enormous black cauldron. One of them is holding a frog, and in the soup they're making floats an eyeball.

"This book is GROSS," I tell Dusty informatively, and then I start to read.

"'Double, double, toil and trouble,'" I announce at breakfast the next morning.

"'Fire burn and cauldron bubble,'" Mom responds, smiling and pouring milk onto bowls of sliced bananas and granola. I gape.

"What*ever*," Dexter says.

At school, before class starts, I ask my teacher, Mr. Chen, if I can borrow the big dictionary that stands on his desk.

"Sure, Edie," he says, setting it down for me with a satisfying *chunk*. "What are you looking up?"

"Newt," I say, frowning over the tissue-thin pages.

"Edie is a newt!" yells Timmy Digby, who is in my class—why? why?—for the third year in a row. "Edie-Snow-Peadie!"

"Settle down, class," Mr. Chen says. "Time for French."

Reluctantly, I go to my seat. Then I pull out my French/English dictionary. Newt: *triton*. "*Triton*," I whisper. "*Oeil de triton*." The rest of the class recites the alphabet.

Already school seems to go on forever, and it's only the second week of September.

At lunch, I eat my sandwich and carrots with my friend Sam. When we're bigger, we decide, we'll go to Africa to see the wildlife. We'll rent a car and drive alongside the zebras and the antelope. We'll take a cooler of food. I've decided not to mention witchcraft to any of my friends just yet, but it's hard to concentrate on other subjects. After lunch, Mr. Chen makes us line up so we can walk neatly down the hall to the library. I squirm with impatience. MY GRANDPA IS

LOSING HIS MIND, I think. BUT THERE MIGHT BE A WAY I CAN HELP. My thoughts feel as bright as fluorescent lights. I wonder if eventually they'll start glowing through my forehead, searing the words and sentences for everyone to see.

My classmates arrange themselves on chairs. I jiggle. Ms. Conklin, the librarian, who has red hair and a red face and speckled reddish skin on her arms, tells us today we're going to start Projects. The class groans. We'll have to find our own books, make notes on index cards, include maps or drawings or something with colors and create a title page and a bibliography. Today is for Brainstorming: we each have to come up with a subject. At the end of the hour, we'll tell our teacher our topics.

I run right over to Mr. Chen. I'm first. "Yes, Edie," he says.

"Witchcraft," I say.

"You have an hour to think about it," Mr. Chen says.

"Witchcraft," I say.

"Edie Snow," Mr. Chen says, shrugging and making a note in his folder. "Witchcraft."

"YES!" I say.

Everybody frowns and tells me to shush.

"I *must* go to the public library," I announce to Mom when I get home from school.

"*Must* you?" she asks. "Well, maybe this evening. I can't drive you right now because I have to take Dex to the mall for shoes. Coming?"

"No!" I say, shuddering.

"Don't answer the phone and don't answer the door."

"I know," I say.

"I know you know, but it makes me feel better to say it anyway," Mom says, giving me a hug.

The big difference between me and girls in books is that they're allowed to go outside. Those girls live in small towns surrounded by hills and babbling brooks and red-gold deciduous woods. Coquitlam, the suburb of Vancouver where I live, is paved as far as the eye can see, and the trees are huge, lone, unclimbable firs and cedars dripping rain. Those girls live in towns that have one of everything: one church, one school, one haunted mansion, one movie-house, one street of stores, one zoo, one library, one museum. You can get anywhere you want by walking, and you know everybody, and you can go places all on your own, even if you're only eleven. In Coquitlam there are three Safeways and a Save-On-Foods, five swimming pools, three skating rinks, ten schools and two shopping malls, but nobody walks anywhere. You don't walk home from school;

you get a ride in somebody's car pool. You have to take the car to buy a Popsicle or mail a letter. In those storybook towns, in the fall there are apple trees with crispy leaves, and mysterious strangers arriving at dusk, and candlelight flickering in the windows of abandoned houses. In winter there's snow and ice-skating and caroling and sleigh rides. In spring there are flowers, and in summer there are more flowers and swimming holes and homemade lemonade.

In Coquitlam, it rains or it doesn't. Those are the seasons. And even if it's sunny, eleven-year-old girls absolutely do not play outside by themselves. That's just how it is.

I wait until after supper, when Mom has done the dishes, tidied up the living room, put on a load of laundry and sat down in front of the TV, to remind her about the library.

"Oh, Edie," Mom says. "Maybe tomorrow."

I think I'm going to explode.

"I'll take you," Dad offers.

That's just ridiculous. "You have never been to the library, and you don't even know where it is," I object.

He frowns, like I've made a good point. "You can drive."

"This is serious!"

"It is?" he says. "Okay. If we're not back in a week, send a search party."

"Better make it two weeks," Mom says. "If it's serious."

They're laughing at me. Now, if I were a witch, what would I do with them? I would point my finger and—what?

"What?" Dad says, because I'm standing still, staring at him, struck by a whole new idea.

Going places with Dad is different from going places with Mom. He plays the radio in the car, for one thing, and he's always trying to be funny. Sometimes I'm in the mood for this, but sometimes, like tonight, I have more important things on my mind.

"What did the elephant say to the gas-station attendant?" he's saying now.

"Yes," I say, distracted. If Grandma is a witch, doesn't that make me at least one-quarter witch? Or is it one-eighth? And even one-eighth ought to be enough for a spell or two, oughtn't it? There was that Great Scientists book on the guy who grew sweet peas, Mendel, who figured out whether you would have blue eyes if your grandparents did, or something. Genetics that's called. I'll have to find that book too.

"'Yes'?" Dad says. "The elephant said 'yes'?"

At the library, I ditch him immediately and go straight to the computer terminal to check the online catalogues. Then I hit the shelves, list in hand. It's a great relief, finally, to be where the information is, getting some real work done.

Fifteen minutes before closing, I stagger over to Dad with a stack of books that comes up to my chin. He's sitting in the Mr. Grasshopper Reading Corner, reading a newspaper. "Help," I say.

"You're kidding," he says. I drop a few books and he picks them up, glancing at their titles. "*Macbeth*?" he says. "*The Salem Witch Trials*?"

"School project," I say.

"Is that a cookbook?"

"It's a herb book," I say warily.

"Can you check my book out on your card too?"

His book is a hardcover, about four inches thick, with no pictures. It's called *Disraeli*. Almost all of my books have a green dot on the spine, meaning they're for younger readers. His book has a fancy letter B on it.

"Am I allowed?"

"We'll just slip it in with these others." Dad squints and shifts his eyes around like a spy. "Tell no one," he says. "If I am captured, eat your library card."

"Dad," I say.

"They won't take us alive!"

"Dad!" I say.

At the counter, the librarian says, "Wow."

"Act normal," Dad says, winking and waggling his eyebrows.

"What are you doing?" the librarian says.

"Research," I say grimly, pushing Dad through the security arch.

Eye of newt, I decide, is going to be a problem.

> *Fillet of a fenny snake,*
> *In the cauldron boil and bake;*
> *Eye of newt and toe of frog,*
> *Wool of bat and tongue of dog...*

On second thought, maybe I should start with something easier than a "charm of powerful trouble," which makes me feel queasy anyway. I get into enough powerful trouble without dragging dismembered amphibians into it, and I like dogs—even their tongues.

I sit on my bed, surrounded by books. So far, the herb book seems the most promising. It tells you how to cure a headache, ease a cough and purify the skin with things like peppermint and marigold. Fine. But it doesn't tell you how to make things happen— how to *cause* a headache, for instance, not to mention how to break a wineglass. But then, if you could find out how to do it from a book, surely people would be casting spells more often. So there has to be some secret element, something I'm missing. Not knowing what else to do, I keep reading. I read about gathering plants by midsummer moonlight. Well, that's out— it's September, and my bedtime is nine o'clock sharp. I read about the town in America where they burned witches at the stake four hundred years ago. But the book thinks they weren't real witches, just smart annoying women who got on people's nerves, and what killed them was not fire so much as smoke inhalation. "Come *on*," I say, impatient. I read about curses. That seems more promising, but the books are maddeningly vague. There's something about burying the hair of your enemy in a secret place, along with a cherished object, and whispering a secret formula.

I look up "cherished" in the dictionary. Then I go to the bathroom.

Dexter's hairbrush lies on the counter next to the sink. People think Dexter is pretty, and Dexter thinks so too. She spends hours in front of the mirror, brushing her hair and looking at her teeth and watching herself blink and breathe. She leaves grungy spots on the mirror, that's how close she stands. Normally this is very aggravating, especially when I have to pee, but the advantage for an apprentice witch is that it leaves an awful lot of useful pale yellow hairs in the brush. I pick out a few long ones, wrap them in a piece of toilet paper and put them in my pocket.

My thinking is, I can't make any mistakes on Grandpa, but I can practice on Dexter. Isn't that reasonable?

The next step, a cherished object, is trickier. That means a dangerous journey to a dark, forbidden land: Dexter's bedroom. I slip from the bathroom, stealthy as an assassin, and glance up and down the hall. The coast is clear. At the entrance to the Cave of Doom I pause, pressing my ear against the door, but all is silent. It's now or never.

BRATS AND CATS KEEP OUT!!!!!!!!!!! The sign on the door is plastered at Edie-height. I ignore it. I turn the handle as quietly as possible, in case Dex is lying on the bed with the headphones on, oblivious to intruding witches. But the light is off and the room is empty. She must not be home from school yet.

Dexter's room is tidy, like mine—we're sisters, after all—and one wall is completely lined with books. But there the similarities end. First of all, the walls

are pink. Pink! There's a full-length tilting mirror on a
fancy iron stand in one corner, ruffled curtains, tasseled
cushions on the bed and three pairs of ballet slippers
in a row under the window, silk ribbons tucked neatly
inside. CDs line the sill. But the biggest difference is
the closet. One door, its catch broken, swings slightly
open, revealing Dexter's greatest preoccupation of all:
clothes. The closet's stuffed, as stuffed and bulging as
a burger on a TV commercial. These, surely, are her
most cherished objects, but somehow I can't imagine
stealing and burying one of Dex's umpteen sweaters.
Maybe something smaller?

I've barely taken a step toward the closet when I
hear voices.

"You know who is cute?" says a voice: Mean Megan.
Oh no. "Tyler is cute."

"He is not," Dexter says. The voices are coming
closer. Dexter's middle school lets out later than my
elementary. Mean Megan must have come home with
Dex to hang out for a while. That means, usually, sitting
on her bed, listening to music, having long private
discussions and telling me to get lost.

"Is too."

"Is not."

"Is!"

"Not!"

The difference between friends and sisters, I reflect as I hurriedly tuck myself inside the closet—there's nowhere else to go—is that friends enjoy the arguing.

"Close the door so my little brat sister doesn't come poking her nose in," Dexter says. They're in the room now. I can't see a thing, but I hear something heavy land on the bed. Knapsack maybe. "She is *so* annoying."

"The next time she bugs you, you should steal her night-light," Mean Megan says. They giggle. "Shred her precious peacock feathers!" Mean Megan says, as Dexter shrieks with laughter. "Poison her cat!"

That's it. When I figure out my powers, these two are toast.

"Don't make me laugh so hard," Dexter says. "It makes my stomach hurt even more."

"I know what you mean," Mean Megan says. Half listening, I start quietly feeling around in the closet. Something small, I think.

"You know how to get someone to like you?" Mean Megan says. I hesitate. My hand has just closed over something hard in a coat pocket. "First, you need something of theirs, something they've touched or carried around a lot."

WAIT A MINUTE HERE.

"And three candles and a small mirror."

"What*ever*," Dexter says doubtfully.

Breathlessly, I stick the little hard thing, whatever it is, in my pocket. The clothes around me rustle with my movement, making the closet door creak.

"What was that?" Mean Megan says.

"Closet," Dexter says. "It doesn't close right. It always does that."

"I know who already likes you anyway."

"Do not."

"Do too."

"Not!"

"Too!"

"Let's go get a snack."

"Okay."

OH FOR PETE'S SAKE, I think. What about the spell? And how does Mean Megan know a spell anyway, even if it is just a lame love spell? Still, I don't have time to think about it now. As soon as I hear their voices fade off down the hallway, I slip from the closet, ready to make my escape. But then I hesitate again. On the bed, half unzipped, lies Mean Megan's blue denim pack. If that isn't fate bopping me on the nose, I don't know what is. A few long hairs cling to the straps like long black threads: perfect. I also take a bright red felt pen that, even capped, smells strongly of cherries. I don't know if Mean Megan cherishes it, but something about "cherry" and "cherish" makes it seem appropriate enough.

And (borrowing from the interesting new information I've just picked up) she certainly carries it around all day and probably touches it a lot too. My pocket isn't big enough for the pen so I stick it in my sock, where it digs rigidly into my ankle, like a splint. I'm bending down to adjust the hem of my jeans over it when the back of my neck starts to prickle. Slowly, I turn around.

Dexter and Mean Megan are standing in the doorway, holding glasses of juice. Dexter is also holding three swirly-striped cupcake candles.

"WHAT ARE YOU DOING IN HERE?" she says.

"LOOKING FOR DUSTY!" I say. Both of us tend to get loud when we're surprised.

"Tell you what," Mean Megan says as I sidle toward the door. "If I see your buggy, mangy, flea-bag, rodent-breath cat, I'll let you know. I'll drown it in the sink and leave it on your pillow." She pushes the knapsack onto the floor and sits down on the bed. So she hasn't noticed anything. I feel the cherry pen slip over the knob of my ankle-bone and poke at my pants. Dexter is still glaring.

"Why do you have candles?" I ask innocently, to distract her. "Did Mom let you?"

It works. "If you tell, I will kill you."

"Ooh." I've made it out the door. "Scary."

"I'll bake chunky cat cookies and make you eat them," Mean Megan says. I see her flip her long black hair over her shoulder just before Dexter slams her bedroom door. Although I can't feel them, I know I hold a few of those same hairs in my tightly clenched fist.

Up in my room, Dusty lies dozing in a lozenge of sunlight on the quilt. "Wake up," I tell him, dumping my loot onto my little desk. "You have to help me. You're my familiar."

Dusty gives his rumbling purr, a loud noise from a small cat.

"That's right," I say busily, getting organized. "You're a witch's cat now."

The thing I pulled from my sister's coat pocket turns out to be a tube of pink lipstick. This is strictly forbidden, so Dexter must cherish it very much to risk the kind of trouble she'll get into if Mom finds it. I wrap the yellow hairs around it and knot them and do the same with the black hairs and the pen. Since I can't go anywhere distant and secret to bury them, I settle on the garbage can by the back door. We empty the smaller kitchen garbage there as it fills up each day, until the men come to dump it into the truck and take it to the landfill.

That's burial, even if it is a few steps removed. When it's my turn to do the trash, I simply add the items, whisper "*Oeil de triton*" thirteen times (my own creation), dump the regular garbage on top and go back inside.

"Mom, I feel terrible," Dexter complains the next morning at breakfast.

"You do?" I say intently. Dexter leans over to flick me in the head.

One night we go to Grandma and Grandpa's house for supper. Usually Grandma makes what Dad calls a royal spread: little dishes all over the table, using all kinds of ingredients I've barely heard of—tamarind, nori, pine nuts, jicama, saffron. Each thing is just one or two bites and is delicious, and you get to eat about thirty things before you're full. Tonight, though, we bring supper with us: three large pizzas and two tubs of ice cream because Dexter and I couldn't agree on just one flavor. Mom says we're making things easy because Grandma is just a tiny, tiny bit tired. I think Mom is a tiny, tiny bit overdoing the nonchalance, which is a word I've recently learned that means pretending nothing is wrong. Pizza in Grandma's house is the definition of wrong.

But when Grandma opens the door, she just says we're all darlings. The dining table is laid with knives and forks and wine glasses and linen and nice china.

"I've never eaten pizza with a knife and fork before," Dad teases Grandma when we're all sitting at the table.

"This is delicious," Grandma says, ignoring him. "What do you call this kind?"

"Hawaiian," Dexter says.

"Do you remember when we were in Hawaii, Harvey?" Grandma asks Grandpa.

We all stop chewing and look at Grandpa.

"Nineteen sixty-four," Grandpa says. "We climbed a volcano and went surfing. Your grandma had a white bathing suit and sunglasses with big white frames, and everyone thought she must be a movie star."

We all start chewing again.

"And this one?" Grandma says, taking another slice. She's only had a couple of bites of her Hawaiian, but who's going to tell her to finish it?

"Italian Meat-Lovers' Special," Dad says. This is his favorite.

Grandma slices off a tiny bite with her knife and puts it in her mouth with her fork. After she swallows, she says, "Isn't that interesting. I don't remember eating anything like that when we were in Italy, do you, Harvey?"

"Nineteen eighty-one," Grandpa says. "All those stray cats in the Foro Romano. I tried to pet one and it bit me and we had to go to a clinic for a tetanus shot, and the nurses all looked like movie stars. At the restaurant that night we ordered white truffle risotto because my hand was so bandaged up I couldn't hold my knife to cut my food."

"Try this one, Grandma," I say, pointing at the third box, my favorite. "It's butter chicken."

"Curried pizza?" Grandma says. I think she's gone a little pale, but by candlelight it's hard to tell. "I'll put a slice aside for my lunch tomorrow, Edie love," she says. "I don't think I could eat another bite right now."

"India," Grandpa says. "Nineteen seventy-six. We got parasites. We couldn't for the life of us figure out why the bathroom had two toilets side by side, but we sure were grateful in the end."

When I get it, I laugh and clap my hands. Dexter pushes her plate away. "Where were you, Dad?" I ask. "Did you get to go to India?"

"Not that trip," Dad says. "But I remember lots of other great trips we took together. Mexico, New York, Australia."

"Aw!" Dexter says, jealous.

"You were never in Australia," Grandpa says, helping himself to another slice. He seems happy now, remembering. "That was just me and your Grandma. She had a white bathing suit and sunglasses with big white frames, and everyone thought she must be a movie star. We tried to go surfing, but the beach was closed because of a shark sighting."

"I know!" Dad says. "I spent the whole morning on the beach with binoculars, trying to see the shark."

"I'll tell you who was with us that trip," Grandpa says. "James. James was there. He would have been, what, about twelve? We had a good time, the three of us."

James is my Dad's name.

"Butter chicken," Grandpa says with relish, taking another bite. "Did you say that was your favorite, Albert? Have to write that down. I think it's my favorite too."

Grandma excuses herself from the table. Mom goes after her.

After supper, Dexter and I clean up without being asked. The only downside to dinner in Grandma's house is that you have to do all the dishes by hand because they're too old and fragile and special for the dishwasher.

"Grandma was crying," Dexter says. She's washing.

"Maybe she's sick," I say. I'm drying. "She barely ate any supper."

"Don't be dumb," Dexter says. "She's exhausted. I heard Dad telling Mom. Grandpa keeps forgetting more and more things, and Grandma's afraid to leave him alone in case he lets the bathtub overflow or forgets to turn the stove off and burns the house down."

"That must be why—" I say, but then I remember to stop myself. Fortunately, Dad comes into the kitchen right at that moment.

"Ice cream!" he says. He's doing that hearty thing again that makes his voice go all strained and funny. "What have we got?"

"Where's Mom and Grandma?" I ask.

"Everyone's in the living room," Dad says. "I'm the ice-cream man, taking orders. You girls leave the rest and go sit with them. It's my turn to do something. What do you think, a scoop of each for everybody?"

In the living room, Mom is looking through a photo album with Grandpa while Grandma watches. Grandma's face looks fine, but she's holding a tissue in her hand and touching it to her nose every now and then. She smiles when she sees us, and when I get close I see her eyes are red. Tired: that must be why she can't cure Grandpa with a spell herself. Being tired probably weakens her powers.

"Look at this, Albert," Grandpa says. He gives the photo album to Mom and reaches up to the shelf behind him for a little figurine. Grandparents' houses are supposed to be all frilly and stuffed with old-fashioned furniture and lace curtains, but not my grandma and grandpa's.

Instead, their house is full of things they've collected on their travels: tropical wood furniture with carvings all over, masks, colorful pottery, brass elephants, rugs with geometric patterns, and little figurines everywhere, like the one Grandpa is showing me.

I take it from his hand: a tiny person carved roughly out of some black wood, about as long as my little finger.

"It's from Haiti," Grandpa says. "They use figures like this to cast spells on people. They burn them or stick them with pins. Your grandma didn't want me to buy it, but I just thought she was pretty."

"How do you know it's a girl?" I ask. The figure looks unfinished and could be any sex or age.

"In my mind, she's a girl," Grandpa says. He rubs the little figure's head affectionately with his thumb. "That was our honeymoon, your grandma's and mine. My favorite trip of all."

"I'm not sure about this," Dad says, coming into the room with a big tray full of ice-cream bowls. "Cherry Garcia and green tea sorbet?" Everyone looks at me.

"We've never had it before!" I say. "I was curious!"

While they're all leaning forward to take their bowls, I put the figurine in my pocket. When it's time for us to leave, I don't put it back.

Over the next few weeks, I improvise more. I decide a spell's power comes from the person performing it, not the formula. If you're a real witch, you can invent variations to suit your purposes. But if you don't have it in your blood, all the toads' tongues and bats' fillets in the world won't help you. And I'm convinced I have it in my blood. About a week after my first success with Dexter, I learn that Mean Megan's parents let her miss an entire day of school for the very same reason: cramps. Dexter explains this to Mom as though it's very significant and she should be taking notes.

"Different people are different" is all Mom will say, but privately, I rejoice. I start collecting ingredients that might come in handy for future spells—spices snuck from the kitchen, a handful of early fall leaves from the schoolyard, black wool and pins from Mom's sewing box, a couple of clean chicken bones left over from supper and, yes, candles from the kitchen drawer next to the knives and forks. My own little cupboard slowly becomes a trove of such odds and ends. And I practice, though not always with success. I crayon a picture of Timmy Digby and poke it full of pinholes. But instead of coming down with chicken pox or bubonic plague, there he is at school the next morning, as grinning and hateful as ever. I have to satisfy myself with the thought that he might have suffered horrible pains at the time I was mutilating my drawing, but went on to a full overnight recovery. For a change, I try a good spell. Carefully, I tip pinches of nicer-smelling spices, like nutmeg and cinnamon, into a spiral seashell I collected from the beach two summers ago—a cherished object of my own. I add one of my own brown hairs and throw it in the garbage, whispering "Dusty" thirteen times. This, I decide, is a spell to keep me out of trouble. And it works too, or seems to. Of course, it's also possible that I'm getting in less trouble these days because I spend all my time in my room, burning through my homework so I can get on with my private studies. It's hard to know.

Other spells are flat-out flops. I completely fail to make Mr. Chen get sick the day of our math test. But that might be because I felt so guilty about taking the piece of chalk from his desk that I put it back the same day without using it at all. I doubt Mr. Chen cherishes his chalk anyway. I fail to make myself invisible. And, after the first time, I fail even to give Dexter more cramps. The whole situation is starting to get frustrating, when Grandma and Grandpa come for another visit.

When I get home after school, I see the familiar chocolate brown station wagon in the driveway. Grandma is sitting in the kitchen with Mom, having a cup of tea.

"Here's my Edie," Grandma says, giving me a hug.

I have a lot of questions. But somehow I don't know how to start asking, especially not with Mom sitting right there.

"Edie's very quiet," Grandma says. "What is it, Edie?"

"Where's Grandpa?" I ask.

"Watching TV," Mom says.

"When is Halloween?" I ask.

"Three weeks," Mom says. "Have you picked a costume?"

"Witch," I say, looking straight at Grandma. But all Grandma says is "Hello, Dexter, dear."

Dexter stands in the doorway in her leotard. "You can't be a witch," she says. "Megan and I are doing costumes together this year. She's going to be a bad witch and I'm going to be a good witch. We already asked, didn't we, Mom?"

I feel panicky. "I have to be a witch!" I say. Halloween is the one day of the year when a spell worth its salt should work, and I can't imagine curing Grandpa dressed as a fairy princess or a pop can or something. And the worst thing is that I can already imagine how perfect the two of them will look together: Megan with her black bad witch's hair and angry black eyes, dressed all in black, and Dexter, the good witch, with her blue eyes and pale yellow hair, dressed in white. The idea is so right, I know no one will be able to resist.

"I'll be a different color witch from them," I say, thinking fast. "I'll be a blue witch. And I won't go trick-or-treating with them or be seen with them."

"Trick-or-treating," Dexter scoffs. "We're too old for that. We're going to a party."

I look desperately at Grandma.

"What a lot of witches this year" is all Grandma says.

Disturbing things are starting to happen. For instance, a boy phones Dexter. This in itself is not totally new, but I hover around long enough, eavesdropping, to hear Dexter call Mean Megan immediately after the boy hangs up. "It worked!" she says.

Which means Mean Megan—no! not Mean Megan!—is a witch too. And if she's teaching Dexter, that means—oh no! no! And, sure enough—

"Mom, Edie's been in my room."

"Was not!"

"Things are, like, rearranged. I think she took something."

"What?" Mom asks.

Of course Dexter can't say what. But she gives me the witchiest look of all time, and I know she knows.

And I was so quiet! I shiver at my sister's uncanny knowledge.

More strangeness: the week before Halloween, Dad comes home from work with the news that he's been given a raise. He looks happier than he has in a while, and I can't help thinking of his disposable razor that I knotted with a hair from his comb and sprinkled with some coffee grounds. He cherishes coffee. I thought I ought to do something nice for him, since he's been rubbing his forehead so much lately and acting so distracted. It wasn't exactly a raise I had in mind, but maybe I can take a bit of the credit. You never know.

Meanwhile, Mom and Grandma are busy making the three witch costumes out of a white bedsheet, a blue bedsheet and some satiny black stuff Mean Megan's mom bought. Mean Megan's mom doesn't know how to sew or is too busy or something. Mom says she feels sorry for Mean Megan.

"You are insane," I tell her. Then I get sent to my room, just like old times.

Halloween finally arrives. The minute I get home from school, I tear out of my clothes and into my costume. I want to put the makeup on right away too, but Mom tells me it would be better to wait until after supper; otherwise I might get blue face-paint in my spaghetti.

"We're having spaghetti? I love spaghetti!" I shout, even though we always have spaghetti on Halloween.

Dexter sits in her prissy room doing homework. She refuses to get dressed up until after supper. "Spaghetti? White costume? Hello?" she says when I bug her.

I can't wait any longer. I run up to my room and retrieve the figurine I took from Grandma and Grandpa's house from my sock drawer. I had it tucked inside a sock to keep it warm. If you can harm someone by abusing a little figure like this, you must be able to help him too, by treating it nicely. For me, the figurine is Grandpa. In the herb book, I found a recipe for clarifying the skin by washing it with an orange and rosemary infusion. Every day, I've been rubbing the figurine's head with a little of my breakfast orange juice and a sprig of dried rosemary I stole from the kitchen. Clarifying the skin can't be all that different from clarifying the mind, can it? I talk to the figurine and rub it and keep it warm in its sock. It's getting a little sticky, probably from the orange juice, but otherwise it seems fine. Since it's a cherished object of Grandpa's, I decide to roll two spells into one for extra power. It's sad how easy it was to get one of his hairs. The day he and Grandma were visiting, I pretended I wanted to give him barrettes, like I used to when I was little, and just pulled one out.

He grunted a little but didn't say anything, just kept watching his golf. He's like a dog that way: friendly but not curious. Cats are different.

Now I wrap the figurine up warmly in an old sock and give it a kiss. I dart down to the back door, stuff the bundle in the garbage and recite the entire witches' scene from *Macbeth*, which I've memorized specially for this occasion. "*Oeil de triton*," I add quickly, slamming down the lid as the door opens behind me.

"What are you doing?" Mom asks suspiciously. "Are you talking to somebody out here?"

"Is it time for trick-or-treating?" I ask.

"It's time for supper."

After supper, Mom paints my face blue, and Sam and I go door to door in our neighborhood. "Trick or treat," I say dutifully, over and over, holding out my plastic pumpkin, not really paying attention. Sam, who is dressed as a chandelier, keeps dropping the battery pack that keeps her lit up and is too preoccupied trying to keep her costume together to notice how impatient I'm getting. Back at home, Grandma and Grandpa will be waiting. They come every year to take pictures of us in our costumes.

"Had enough?" Sam asks.

"'Thrice the brinded cat hath mew'd. Thrice and once the hedge-pig whin'd. Harpier cries: 'tis time, 'tis time.' Let's hit the road," I say. Sam shrugs and her lights go out again.

When we get home, though, only my parents are waiting. Mom starts to say something about Grandma not wanting Grandpa to drive and Grandpa refusing to come. Dad's on the phone in the den, where I can't overhear.

"What happened?" I ask.

"Grandpa wasn't feeling well," Mom says. "They decided to stay home this year. I'll take a picture of you and we can e-mail it to them, how's that?"

When she's gone into the den to download the picture from the camera to the computer—in other words, to talk to Dad without me hearing—I sneak out to the garbage can by the back deck and retrieve my old sock. It's now slightly spaghetti-stained from our plate scrapings. I'll wipe the stickiness off and put the figurine back the next time we go to Grandma and Grandpa's house. Something tells me Grandpa won't have noticed it was ever gone.

The day after Halloween, I find out I got an A+ on my school project. *Exceptional work, Edie!* Mr. Chen wrote on it in red. He even asks me to read it aloud to the class. When I get home from school, I find out Dexter is grounded because when Mom went to pick her up from the party the night before, she got there early and found Dex wearing makeup borrowed from Mean Megan. Not Halloween makeup, but the other kind, which Dexter isn't allowed until she's fifteen. Mom says Dexter knew she was breaking the rules, so now she has to Suffer the Consequences. Mean Megan is in the doghouse too and isn't allowed to come over for the entire month of November. And then, when I'm tidying up my closet (throwing out the leaves and bones, restoring the pins to Mom's sewing box, stacking the library books it's time to return, and wondering what to do with the spices), I find the lucky nickel Grandpa gave me weeks ago. That means I still have a wish saved, to use any way I want the next time I see a fountain.

Or I could put it in my savings jar. I think that's what I'd rather do. It's not much, but even the tiniest little bit is something to hold onto. Like Grandpa remembering what kind of pizza I like or where he went on his honeymoon. That's not nothing, is it?

Stupid Christmas

"Stupid Christmas," I say.

"Edith Jasmine Snow." Mom makes her raisin face. "You are coming with Dexter and me to the mall for Christmas shopping and I am not going to hear one more word about it."

"But," I say.

"Not one word!"

"*Oh*," I say, feeling incredibly frustrated; then I start coughing again.

"Cough away from me," Dexter says, flapping her hands. We're sitting in the kitchen having an unreasonably early Saturday morning breakfast because of Mom's big plans for the day. "You're infectious."

I lean over and cough on her.

"Edith," Mom says sternly, and I know if I weren't sick and Mom didn't want to get moving, I would be shot into my room like a cannonball. Here's what's wrong with me: coughing, sneezing, runny nose, achy head and a throat like I've swallowed sand. The only neat part is my voice, which has gone deep. I keep trying to sing, but that only makes my cough worse. I give up on breakfast, pushing my toast away. It's too painful.

"Oh, Edie." Mom isn't angry, though. She smoothes my hair back and holds her palm to my forehead for a minute. Then she goes to the cupboard and gets the cough syrup and the aspirin.

"*Oh*," I wail again. I hate swallowing pills. "Can't I stay home?"

"Yeah," Dexter says.

"No, because Daddy is away all day today and I don't want you spending the day alone." Dad is working on a Major Presentation for an Important Client and is Putting In Some Serious Overtime because his firm is Down To The Wire. He left the house before any of us was up, leaving as evidence only a coffee mug in the sink.

Mom feeds me two swollen spoonfuls of thick, sharp, sweet cough syrup, supposedly raspberry. More like mutant raspberries, I think, shaking my head to dispel the taste. More like raspberries from a tender clump in a quiet corner of a nuclear power plant that one day—or night, it would be at night, with only a janitor around as witness—grow to seven hundred times their normal size. They sprout arms and legs and faces and powers and personalities. They start wearing capes, and letters on their berry chests, and going on evil adventures before falling into giant vats of boiling cough mixture, all thanks to the effects of nuclear radiation. (I don't know what nuclear radiation is, but I do watch cartoons, and the syrup does taste absolutely terrible without entirely losing touch with a certain recognizable berry-like flavour.) "Now take your pill," Mom says.

Pills are just plain mean. They stick in your throat and make you gag on their bitterness. They don't have personalities.

"Hurry up, Edie," Dex says bossily. "I have to get cards and presents for all my friends. I want to find something special for Grandpa. I have *so much* to do." For a second she sounds just like Mom, sort of flustered and distracted and satisfied all at the same time. She speaks as though she isn't really talking to me at all but rather to some invisible person, someone she's showing off for. Who could that be? I remember the ancient gods and goddesses we're learning about in social studies, how they can appear or disappear or turn into whatever they want. Maybe Dexter thinks some of them are listening, disguised as toasters and microwaves and yellow kitchen curtains with blue flowers. Typical Dexter, to imagine such amazing and powerful beings would be interested in her stinky little shopping trip.

"Have you taken that pill yet?" Mom asks.

"Almost." Dusty pours around the corner and starts mewing in front of his empty food bowl. I jump up. The ancient Egyptians worshipped cats. I find the ancient Egyptians very sympathetic.

"Ah!" Mom says sharply, pointing at my pill. I clap it into my mouth, wince, swallow and gulp at my water. Then I take a scoop of cat food from the bin and put it in Dusty's bowl. I love feeding my cat. "Don't pet him while he's eating," Mom says, although I don't know why not. Dusty doesn't mind, he just keeps eating. "Go brush your teeth and put your shoes on."

"I'm bored already," I say. Dexter is waiting by the front door with her jacket on and her little purse strap looped across her chest. "How much money do I have?" I ask. "I want to get something special for Grandpa too." I haven't been allowed to visit Grandma and Grandpa since I got sick. I don't like to think about the reason why: Grandpa is so weak that my cold might land him back in hospital. Those were Dad's exact words, like he was trying to make me feel guilty.

It's getting harder to think about Grandpa without a little knot of hurt in my chest. Something is coming, I keep thinking, something not so good. At the same time, I can't imagine anything changing. Grandpa will always be Grandpa, calling me Albert and letting me do stuff no one else does, like starting his car by turning the key while he presses the gas, or tasting his drink.

"Now do you see why little girls don't get beer?" he said after I spluttered it straight back out, but he said it nicely. When I asked him if letting me have a taste was a secret, he said, "No, no, no. You never have secrets from your mom and dad. If anyone will get in trouble, it will be Grandpa, not you." He was right, too. Dad yelled at him, but he didn't care. "Albert was curious, just like I was at her age" was all he said. "It's good to be curious."

I wonder if maybe that's the problem: he's gotten so old and tired that things don't make him curious anymore, and that makes him grumpy and sad. I decide to find him a present that will make him curious again, something more special than Dexter could ever dream of. "Can I go to the bank?" I ask Mom.

"Not today," she says. "You have all those loonies in your jar."

"That's my pirate treasure," I complain. Dexter snorts. "You snorted," I tell her.

"Teeth," Mom says, pointing.

In the bathroom, I squeeze gel paste onto my toothbrush and brush slowly, trying to stare up into the tube. Could an ancient god fit into there? When he turns back into his actual self, would he be all goopy and blue? I know—after all that witch business back at Halloween—there are no such thing as gods and goddesses and magic powers really, but it's still interesting to think about the possibilities. Then Mom and Dex start calling me at the same time. I rinse and gargle and spit and pee and flush and wash my hands and stomp into my shoes and grab my ski jacket and race over to the front door. Then I'm dizzy.

"I get to sit in the front," Dexter says.

"Mommy," I say. My head feels prickly.

"I was ready first," Dexter says.

"I'm sick," I say. Cleverly: "I might puke on the back of your neck."

"Don't say puke," Mom says.

"It's just a word," I say. Dexter gets to sit in front.

The drive to the mall is as familiar as cheese. It's so familiar it makes me sleepy. I know every house and tree. The little purple school that isn't my school because it doesn't have enough French, even though it's closer to home. Wong's corner store. The big woods, called Mundy Park, where Dad and I sometimes go for a walk.

Once we saw rabbits in the woods, but when I got excited they ran away. The windshield wipers suck and slurp at the raindrops that pepper the windscreen. I lean my head back against the head pad in the back seat and wonder about the lives of rabbits. Closing my eyes feels like letting go of a helium balloon. Once I think I hear Mom say, "Ssh, she's asleep," and I wonder who she's talking about.

When we get to the mall I sit up and say, "I want a rabbit."

"And I want a parking spot," Mom says. "You girls help me look."

We drive around the rooftop part and the underground part that echoes, but every space is taken. Cars looking for spaces are going slowly and people are running to and from their parked cars, holding plastic bags over their heads, trying not to get wet. I feel hot. "Mommy," I say, and then I yawn.

"There," Dexter says, stabbing a finger at the windscreen. Ahead of us, a van is backing out of a spot.

"Yes!" I say.

"No," Mom says, because it's a wheelchair spot— we see the white and blue symbol of a wheelchair painted on the ground as we drive by. A couple of spaces later she brakes when she sees a couple loading up their station wagon. They smile and wave at us to show they're leaving as soon as they've packed all their shopping away.

Dexter jiggles up and down in her seat impatiently. Mom catches my eye in the rearview mirror and grins. Dexter is extremely weird about the mall. She loves it. It makes her happier than anything else in the world, and she wants to go there every day. She knows each store and what things she wants from each store. She knows what's a good deal and where you can get a better deal. She knows what food you can get at each of the fast-food counters in the food court and where the elevators are and where to get the best haircut and which stores have mirrors in the change rooms and which don't. She's a mall expert.

"Now," Mom says, but just as the station wagon backs out, a sports car opposite us zips into the spot we've been waiting for. "Ooh," Mom and Dexter say at the same time, with mean squinty looks on their faces that should have made the sports car shrivel up and disappear in a sour little puff of smoke. Instead, a man gets out of the driver's side and walks toward the mall without even glancing at us.

"Mommy," I murmur, watching the man for as long as I can. He's pulled a cell phone out of his pocket and is dialling a number while he walks. I press my hot forehead against the cool window, watching him.

Would Grandpa like a cell phone? One for him and one for me, and we could call each other, like spies?

"That man was so rude," Mom says. "Dex, if I drop you and Edie by the doors, will you look after your sister until I meet you inside? You can go to the card shop and start choosing."

"Yay!" Dexter says, ripping off her seat belt. I follow more slowly. We get out in front of the glass archway that leads into the mall. I watch Mom's car rejoin the circling throng. I feel sleepy again. "Hey, dope," Dex says, "come inside. You're getting wet." I look at her and start coughing and can't stop. I cover my mouth with my hand to keep the germs from flying every-where. Germs, I imagine, are like pepper: tiny black dots in the air. My throat hurts all the way up into my ears.

"You're all red," Dexter says when I finish. Then she does something extraordinary: she holds her hand gently to my forehead the way Mom did at breakfast. "You're, like, way hot," she says. Again, though, I have the feeling she's less interested in me than in the invis-ible watcher. She's just trying to be grown up since Mom left her in charge. So I shrug away from her and say in my clogged, scratchy voice, "OH BY DOD. Doe dutch be." After that, Dexter starts acting normal again, and we ignore each other all the way to the card store.

There's a lot to look at along the way. The mall is all decorated for the holidays, and carols are playing on the loudspeaker. In Center Court is the annual display, Christmas Castle. Dexter and I are both too old for Christmas Castle, where Santa sits on his throne and kids sit on his knee while the photographer takes pictures. We're too old for the toy railroad that goes in circles around Christmas Castle, where little kids scream to get on or get off while teenage girls in green felt mini-skirts and green felt hats chew gum and tell them to get back in line. These girls roll their eyes and pop bubbles and push their hair behind their fake pointy ears. They're elves. One day Dexter will get a job as an elf, I'm pretty sure. She's just as cute and blond and bored as these girls, plus she has good posture from years of ballet. But you have to be in grade ten. Dexter and Mean Megan asked. They're only in grade eight.

I wonder if I will go insane, like Dexter, once I'm thirteen. I wonder how much will have changed by then, two years from now. I start to wonder whether Grandpa will even—but then I have to shut that thought down quickly because it makes my chest hurt too much. Grandpa will always be Grandpa, and right now what I need is to find him the perfect present. That's all.

"Hurry up," Dexter says now because I've slowed down to watch the train while I think. I still like the train a little, even though I'm too big to ride on it. It has a silver bell and wooden benches to sit on. I'm hoping one of the elf girls will see me standing there forlornly (I try to look forlorn) and offer me a free ride, but none does. A boy going past on the caboose makes a face at me and says, "Nah-nah," and calls me a name, and then I hurry to catch up with Dexter. Christmas Castle has changed; it's not as good as it used to be.

An angel flops past over my head, beating big flashing wings, but when I look up, it's vanished. Now that's strange.

I find Dexter in the card shop, picking through a shelf of boxed Christmas cards with two other ladies. There are upside-down cards, spilled boxes and boxes on the floor. It looks like a hurricane hit the cards. The other ladies are talking loudly and moving in on Dexter's space as if she just isn't there. She looks grim.

"I saw an angel," I tell her. I feel kind of hot and woozy.

Dexter gives me a box to hold. It shows a man angel with curly yellow hair and a trumpet and a tree branch and under his feet a big fancy letter G in a gold box, followed by a bunch of tiny letters.

"In the atrium," I say, which is the name for the glass ceiling in the mall. "What does it say?"

"Gloria in Excelsis Deo."

"Eggshells?" I say. Dexter snatches the box back. "Find one with cats," I suggest.

"Oh, go away," Dexter says, stamping her foot.

I wander through the card shop, looking at the posters and mugs and stuffed animals and stickers that fill all the spaces where there aren't cards. My head hurts. Everything seems very bright, even the stuffed animals, which normally I would enjoy petting. There's a little gray elephant that seems to be staring at me in a creepy way. The fluorescent lights buzz loud and dangerous as bees. I hurry out of the store.

There are too many people in the mall. That's the problem. A few less people and I'd be able to concentrate much better. A few less people and no more angels flopping by like big pterodactyls. I whip my head back, thinking I've seen another out of the corner of my eye, but it's only flashing lights from the giant metallic Christmas ornaments that hang from the glass panes in the ceiling. Still, I could swear I heard flapping—air beaten by huge wings. I decide to go back to the doors where we came in and wait for Mom there. I'll tell Mom about the angels, and Mom will be interested, and together we'll watch the miniature train go round and round for as long as we want, and she'll help me think of the perfect thing for Grandpa.

Because I'm not exactly sure where the main doors are, I waste some time following a man and a woman who are carrying handfuls of bags from all different stores. Surely they're leaving. But the woman keeps saying, "Bruce, honey, just in here, honey. Brucie? Bruce? I'm just nipping in here, honey." She just nips in the candle store or the shampoo store or the joke underwear store while the man stands outside, his arms pulled straight by the weight of his bags. He stares at the floor until she comes out with one more bag. His preoccupied look reminds me of the Greek god Zeus staring down from Olympus at the little Greek people below, trying to decide who to zap with a bolt of lightning. Zeus has a wife named Hera.

"Zeussie?" Hera says, emerging from the joke underwear store waving a pair of Rudolph socks with a little red lightbulb on the big toe that lights up when she presses the heel. "Aren't these darling?" No wonder Zeus is so gloomy and destructive. Still, it might be wiser to get out of his way. I'm backing slowly toward Ralph's Shoe Repair U Nixem We Fixem when I'm knocked off my feet and sent flying toward the fountain.

"Are you okay?" a voice says.

At first all I can see of the voice is a pair of running shoes. No, that's not true. At first all I can see are little lit matches, winking and blinking in circles like fireflies, making dizzying patterns between my brain and normal vision. Once they've gone out, reluctantly it seems, one by one, all I can see is a pair of running shoes. I've never seen another pair like them. "Where did you get those cool running shoes?" is more a Dexter line than an Edie line, especially when addressed to a boy closer to Dexter's age than mine, but I try to say it anyway. That's how extraordinary these shoes are. But because I'm still recovering from my collision with the floor, and sitting up has started me coughing again, it comes out in a series of jerky, spluttering and totally incomprehensible syllables.

I use my coughing time to study the shoes more closely. They look like the fastest shoes ever made: they're sleek and sparkling, blue and gold, with a white wing design on each side. I'm not very good at brands (that's Dex's territory), but I could swear I've never seen a pair like them and neither has anyone else. They seem to glow slightly, especially the soles, as though a spotlight shines on them from beneath the floor. They seem to hum or buzz, faintly but distinctly, above the workaday buzz and hum of shoppers cruising around the crowded mall. They even seem (though I can't be quite sure about this) to radiate heat. I'm just reaching out to touch them with my fingertips when their owner grasps me by the armpits, awkwardly but not roughly, and hauls me to my feet.

"Are you okay?" the boy says again. "I'm really sorry about that. I was, ah, delivering this message and I just didn't see you." He's even a little older than Dexter, and his concern for me, I can see, is rapidly cooling as he realizes I'm going to be fine and somebody his own age might see him talking to me. He's a cool kid. Well obviously, in those shoes. Those shoes!

"Delivering a message?" I say thickly. Messages, winged shoes—

"Uh, yeah." The boy glances nervously over his shoulder. "Look. The thing is, if you're okay, I've gotta go. I've gotta catch up with this guy and—"

"Hey, Mark!" A boy standing at the top of the stairway to the mall's upper level is calling down to the boy with the shoes. "Did you make a new friend?"

"I'm gonna get you!" he calls back, shaking his fist. "I hope you're hungry! I'm gonna make you eat this!"

"You and what posse?" the upstairs boy calls down. He's even jumping up and down a little, doing a kind of victory dance, and waggling his fingers rudely.

"What's a posse?" I ask.

"His friends," the boy says grimly, never taking his eyes off his enemy, as though the word "friends" means "extremely hideous, stinky and contemptible sewer rats." "Look, I gotta go," he says again, probably only hesitating because I'm still swaying a little.

"Hi, Mark," another voice says from somewhere behind me.

The effect of this second voice is both astonishing and hilarious. The boy spins around as though someone has pulled him on a string. His face turns pink.

"Hi, Vee," he says, and then he squirms and looks at his feet as though he's just done something mortifying, like pee his pants.

I turn too and see a girl about Dexter's age who is—is it possible? it evidently is, though I've never seen it before—prettier than Dexter. She has curly yellow hair to Dexter's straight, and her brown eyes are as big as—not a rabbit's, and not a doe's, though they have something of both, something soft and warm and appealing. She wears a red skirt and a white T-shirt with a big pink heart on it, which is pretty corny but suits her perfectly. There's something strange about her, something I can't quite put my finger on. It's not just her effect on the boy with the cool shoes, who has turned a few shades pinker and is evidently trying to engage in casual conversation. I've tuned this part of the scene out while I study the girl, and decide to tune back in, if only for the entertainment value.

I've seen boys doing this with my sister, and the results are usually a cross between cringingly embarrassing and extremely hilarious.

"How's it going?" the boy says. He's trying to make his voice go deep but it still has a little squeak of nervousness in it. I repeat his words under my breath just to reassure myself that my flu-voice is deeper than his normal voice. It is.

"I'm shopping," the girl says. Her voice has the same velvety satisfaction as Dexter's when she says phrases like this, anything to do with "mall" or "shopping" or "clothes." "Is that Perry up there? Perry's cool."

"You think everybody's cool," the boy named Mark says. His face goes from pink to red, and he starts to look mad again.

"I have to go," the girl says.

Stammering, the boy offers to buy her a drink at the food court, but she just laughs and flips her hair—a move I've seen Dexter practicing in the mirror—and bounces away. Her hair bounces perfectly and she seems to be walking on balloons. Just before I lose sight of her, I realize what the girl reminds me of and what makes her so strange. She's like a cartoon. Everything about her is perfect and slightly larger than life, but she's too smooth and clear, without any edges. Her skirt has no wrinkles and her hair looks like someone has drawn it with a yellow felt-tip so that no curl will ever be out of place and frizziness is out of the question. Her eyes are too big, like cute animals in Disney movies, and her colors—yellow hair, brown eyes, pink lips, white T-shirt, red skirt—are too even and flawless to be believable. I wonder, if you had a big enough eraser, whether you could just rub her out.

When I turn back to confirm my suspicions with the boy with the cool shoes, he's gone, and so is the boy upstairs. I imagine them zipping after each other so fast they'll leave lines in the air behind them; if one of them ever catches up with the other and bops him on the head, the air above him will explode with little stars and number signs and the word "BANG," written all in capitals.

Something wings past my head, almost brushing my cheek, and I snap around to see what it is, but it's gone. Sometimes pigeons get inside the mall and circle round and round the skylights in the atrium, flapping and pooping and looking for a way out, but I think this was bigger than a pigeon, and it got away too fast. I still haven't found Grandpa's gift, the gift that will wake him up again, turn him back into old Grandpa. Socks that light up? Fast shoes? A pet bird to whiz around his head? I think about being asleep and being awake and the eerie half-place in between, where

Grandpa seems to be stuck. I think again of gods and angels, zipping back and forth between their world and ours, which reminds me of Dexter's Christmas cards, which reminds me of Dexter and Mom. I'd better make another effort to find them before I fall asleep standing up and wake up in the wrong world myself.

Even though I'm not hungry, I decide to try the food court. I know how to get there because it's right in the middle of the mall, and all the different starfish arms and legs of the mall eventually lead back to it. Also, you can simply follow the smell of French fries. Mom and Dex like to stop everything, right in the middle of shopping, and sit down in the food court and have a drink, just when you're finally starting to get things accomplished and know that within another half hour you will be done and be able to get back home to your room and your books. This is enormously aggravating, but it's also where Mom and Dexter start to resemble each other very much. Inevitably I go along with them, after only a token protest, just so I can watch this strange phenomenon. Mom will buy a coffee from the gourmet coffee place, and she'll let Dexter buy a special kind of coffee that's mostly milk. I'll get a strawberry Julius from Orange Julius, which is the juice-place-with-hot-dogs. I suspect that when Mom and Dexter are alone, they sit in the uncomfortable fancy iron garden chairs at a little round marble table, like a dinner plate on a stick, right inside the gourmet coffee shop itself. But when we're all together we aren't allowed, Mom explained, because my Julius was an Outside Drink. That means we have to sit on the molded plastic seating in the middle of the food court at a table where someone has always left the remains of a greasy, salty, ketchuppy lunch. Mom and Dexter will fuss away at the table, cleaning it with dinky paper napkins. Then we'll all sit down together and they'll load their shopping bags on the table and pull out their purchases and exclaim over them, reassuring each other that they've picked the perfect color or type or size.

"Perfect," Mom will say.

"Totally, like, perfect," Dex will say.

"I love it," Mom will say.

"Totally," Dex will say. "Love it, totally. Shut up, Edie."

"Edie, be nice," Mom will say. "Aren't these socks perfect?"

"Totally, like, perfect," Dex will say. It's like when the CD player gets stuck and you listen to the same little blip over and over again, trapped forever, so annoying it's kind of fascinating.

Finally they'll put the things away again and sip their drinks and noodle on about other things they want to buy when they've saved enough money. With Dexter it's usually clothes; with Mom it's usually something for the house: a toaster or a new coffee table. These conversations are incredibly endless and boring, and the two of them listen to each other with such rapt attention that I'm always mesmerized. I can picture them now, chatting away, having completely forgotten about me since they're so wrapped up in their coffees and their talk. This makes me feel pretty sorry for myself—a little weepy, almost—even though at the back of my mind I know they're doing no such thing because they'll be looking for me too.

I find myself following a man walking a dog. The dog walks a little in front of the man and has a fancy harness, and the man walks very tall and straight, without seeming to look around him very much. I can see the dog has a long snout and pointy ears and is very clean. Pets aren't allowed in the mall; that's a rule. I wonder if the dog is not really a dog at all but something more like the Egyptian god Anubis, a being that's only part dog and can get up and walk around on its hind legs and think and talk like a person if he chooses to. Again, in the part of my mind that has stayed cool despite my fever, where I can see my worried mother and sister scouring the mall for me, I also know the dog is a seeing-eye dog and the man holding the harness is blind. Maybe a dog for Grandpa, to help guide him around when he gets mixed up? An extra-powerful god-dog? Everything is getting swirly and mixed up in my mind. It's easy to imagine that there are ancient gods walking through the mall just like they walk across the pages of my social studies book at school. It doesn't help when the stores suddenly all swoon sideways and I abruptly lose my balance and stagger to my left. I bump into someone who says angrily, "Watch where you're going!" and stomps away before my eyes can focus and I can explain that I'm really not feeling very well. I'm only trying to find my Mom, for Pete's sake, already. Give me a break.

The food court is stuffed with moms and dads and teens and squirts of kids and shoppers of all stripes. They're either crowding all the tables with their lunches or clogging up the pathways between the tables and the fast-food kiosks with empty trays, circling like gulls, trying to decide what they want. On the rare occasions when Mom and Dexter and I have lunch here, we always get the same thing: California rolls for Dex, kappa maki for me and dynamite rolls for Mom, all from the sushi place, because Mom believes sushi is more nutritious than fried anything. Almost everything else the food court has to offer is fried something. I'm always powerfully interested in the bento boxes, with their little compartments of rice and salad and teriyaki and tempura and noodles and fruit, but Mom always says that's just Too Much Food.

Too much food. Everywhere I look there's food: food heaped high on trays and in paper boxes, food on tables, food that's fallen to the floor and is getting trampled underfoot. Everywhere people are chewing with bulging cheeks and laughing with their mouths open and licking their fingers and feeding their babies and picking what they don't want out of their lunches and dropping it—pickle slices, onions, tomatoes. The overpowering smells and hideousness of it all makes me feel queasy.

In desperation, I head for the one place in the entire food court where I think I might truly find my mother and sister: the gourmet coffee store. I can't see it clearly from where I'm standing, and I fight my way through the crowds until I can see into the entire shop. There's a long lineup at the counter of people buying bags of coffee beans and painted mugs and gift baskets. But farther back, where the tables are, the chaos gives way to calm. People sit at the little tables in quiet pairs, sipping their drinks, eating nothing, talking quietly, probably about how lucky they are to have found seats inside and how unpleasant it would be to have to sit anywhere else. I have to walk right into the store to see all the way to the back. This makes me feel a little shy since I don't intend to buy anything, but no one seems to be paying any attention to me, and it's such a relief to get away from all that chewing. Right at the back of the shop, at the very last table—Dex's favorite, as it happens, the most secluded, the one behind the palm plant, under the poster of the Eiffel Tower in Paris—sits the largest man I've ever seen. He's taken both chairs from the table and put them side by side so he'll be able to sit properly; that's how big he is. He's sipping from a tiny coffee cup that looks the size of a thimble in his huge hand, and he's laughing quietly to himself, his big face creased, his eyes almost vanished with amusement. In a vase on the table in front of him stands a single white flower, and I know I've found the Buddha.

"Excuse me," I say, because surely he'll know what to get for Grandpa, something perfect and simple and beautiful and calming, to bring him gently back into the world.

My voice is too soft, or the noise from the lineup at the cash register combined with the shop's jazzy music is too loud, and he doesn't seem to notice me at all. He turns the page of the magazine lying flat on the table in front of him (I hadn't noticed it at first) and laughs again at something he reads there.

"Excuse me," I say again.

At the table next to his sits a pair of Indian women in saris, with their hair in neat buns and their feet in sandals. Both of them have diamonds in their noses. They're surrounded by bags of shopping and seem to be going through a list together, crossing off what they've bought. When they hear my voice they look up at me and smile.

"Excuse me," I say, very loudly this time, standing at the Buddha's elbow, and then I start to cough. He looks up at me. Then he gets up from his chairs and goes over to the sleek black table with the milk and cream and half-and-half and soy and white sugar and brown sugar and honey and clear glucose syrup and artificial sweetener and brings back a paper cup of water, which he gives to me. I sip it and the coughing goes away.

"Are you lost?" he asks.

"Is she lost?" one of the Indian women asks.

I start coughing again, and all the tables and chairs and people slip sideways in my vision. I'd fall over but the Buddha puts his hand on my shoulder to make me steady.

"Be still," he says.

Which is exactly what the Buddha would say.

"Where is your mummy?" the Indian woman asks. She has an English accent, like the people who call the tennis matches on TV that Dad likes to watch. Twenty-love, second service. Nice shot, that. Lovely.

"I don't know," I say.

The Buddha closes his magazine. "Should we call security?" he asks the Indian women, as though they're all together and not strangers. This is nice of him, though I'm not sure why.

"Did you come with your mummy today?" the Indian woman asks me again.

"And my sister," I say.

The Buddha nods thoughtfully and says he'll get security. He gets up from his two chairs and tells me I should sit down and wait with the ladies until he gets back. Gratefully I climb up onto one of the chairs, which is warm from his sitting on it. For a minute I close my eyes, and then I start coughing again. The Indian women cluck sympathetically, and one of them reaches over and touches my forehead and clucks some more. Then she starts pulling things out of her shopping bags to show me. I understand the woman is trying to make me smile. She pulls out a pair of socks and tears off the tags and the sticky paper holding them together and slips one over her hand to make it a puppet. She calls the puppet Freddy. Freddy pretends to eat my finger, and then he pretends to sip the woman's coffee. "Oh, oh, oh," the woman says in a funny voice that's supposed to be Freddy's voice. "Tummy ache! Do you have a tummy ache too?"

I shake my head. I know the woman is being nice, and I don't want to risk being rude by telling her I'm too old for sock puppets named Freddy. The woman seems to take the hint, though, because she pops the sock off her hand and back into a bag. From another bag she starts pulling out stuffed animals and explaining these are for her nieces and nephews. "Now, I know you're a big girl," she says. "But can you remember when you were little? Which one would you have liked best?"

Admittedly, this is more interesting. I try to focus on the mounds of plush. There's a bear and a raccoon and a hot pink hippo and a glittery fish. Then, to my horror, the woman pulls out the creepy-eyed gray elephant from the card shop.

"He's so cute," the woman says, pretending to make him walk across the air toward me. "Look at him. Isn't he cute?"

I nod, then shake my head, then blink several times and slide off my chair to the floor, where I land with a thump just before everything goes black.

On Christmas morning, I lie on the sofa while Mom and Dad and Dexter bring my presents over to me. This is a change from the usual rip-roaring, hair-flying, tornado-raising creature that's me under the tree at six thirty in the morning while everyone else struggles to act awake, but I'm still not My Old Self, as Mom puts it.

My new self sleeps in to nine o'clock and then nests on the sofa with a blanket and pillows, gazing sleepily at the blinking lights on the tree more than at the presents under it. Mom and Dad make tea and coffee, and Dexter peels us each a mandarin orange. Dad lights the fire he laid last night, with about as much mumbling under his breath as every year as match after match extinguishes itself with nothing to show for its efforts. Finally the fire catches, blue and then orange, and everyone has something hot in a mug (even I have tea), and Dexter asks me if I want to start and I say no, that's okay, Dexter can start. Then everyone gets concerned again and says they'll bring my presents over to me.

Still, I'm getting better. I'm not nearly as sick as I was in the days immediately after I fell off my chair in the coffee shop and woke up in a bright white room. Mom and Dexter and a man I didn't recognize were leaning over me with worried looks on their faces. "Mommy," I said.

"Hi, sweetie," Mom said. I could see the worry lines on her forehead and between her eyebrows.

"I saw Zeus and Mercury and Ganesh and the Buddha," I said. "Grandpa's in the underworld. Next time I want to try coffee instead of a Julius, like Dex."

"She's delirious," the strange man said. Afterward, Mom told me he was in charge of the mall, and we were in the first-aid room, next to the cinemas, which most people never get to see.

"No she isn't," Dexter said, looking at me closely, but not in a mean way.

After I fainted, the Indian women quickly arranged their coats for me to lie on and put something soft under my head. The big man returned with two security men and a stretcher, and they took me to the little room, where Mom and Dexter had been waiting. They had gone to security as soon as they realized I was missing. After we got home, I had a fever for a few days and got to drink lots of soup and ginger ale, which came out about as fast as it went in. For the first time in the history of the world as I knew it, I didn't help decorate the house but watched from the sofa until I couldn't keep my eyes open. I also fell asleep during my favorite videos, card games, stories and meals.

Still, I slowly got better. My temperature came down and I was finally able to explain coherently about the various ancient gods in the mall. I reassured Mom that I knew they weren't really gods (just as the witches had not really been witches), though they had certainly seemed like gods at the time. Mom seemed to understand. Even Dexter listened to me with unusual attention and refrained from making fun of me. When I quietly pointed this out to Mom, after Dex had gone for one of her sessions in the bathroom, Mom told me I had really been pretty sick and had given everyone Quite A Scare. No one ever asked me what I meant about Grandpa being in the underworld, which made me kind of glad. In the end I just signed my name to the card our whole family sent, to go with a collection of old records Dad found in an antique store. They were a kind of music called swing that Dad said Grandpa loved and would help him remember good times. So I'm not the only one who thinks about these things.

By Christmas morning even my voice is back to normal and all I am is tired. So gift giving, this year, is a staid and proper affair. Gifts are unwrapped decorously, one by one, exclaimed over, and the paper refolded for next year before the next gift is handed out. My favorite gift comes from Dex. This in itself is not all that unusual since—whatever her other faults—Dexter gives considerate presents. But this year, when she hands me a plain envelope, quite small, with just a little drawing of holly in one corner, at first I'm disappointed. What can something as small as my hand and as flat as a sheet of paper possibly contain?

It turns out to contain exactly that: a sheet of paper. Specifically, it's a coupon for a free drink at the coffee shop in the mall.

"What's a lat?" I ask.

"Latt*ay*," Dex says, watching my face to see if I like it. "It's spelled l-a-t-t-e. You pronounce the 'e' like an 'a.' It's coffee with milk, like I always get. You said you wanted to try one like mine next time."

I smile, and Dexter smiles too. Then we go back to ignoring each other because that's less embarrassing.

"I almost forgot," Mom says later, when she's tidying up the last of the ribbons and cards and wrap. "This came for you while you were sick."

It's a Christmas card, still in a sealed envelope, with my name and address and a stamp, meaning it's real mail. I don't get much real mail, except for postcards when Grandma and Grandpa go on holiday.

"Who's it from?" Dexter asks.

I look at the return address. "Robert!" I say.

Dex and Mom look blank.

"You remember," I tell Mom. "In the summer, at the lake. We caught the fish." Then Mom remembers too, but Dex, of course, doesn't know who we're talking about and makes fun of me for getting a card from a boy. As if Robert was what Dex would think of as a boy. Ridiculous.

The card shows a reindeer trying to change the burnt-out red light bulb in his nose while the other reindeer stand around the sleigh, frowning impatiently and tapping their hooves on their hips.

Dear Edie, the card says. *Well, it is Christmas I guess so here is a card. I hope you remember me. If you saw me you might not recognize me anymore. My mom makes me go to Weight Watchers now and I lost twenty pounds. I'm not allowed to eat Christmas treats, only turkey and salad. If you could eat a sugar cookie and think of me, I guess I would like that. Maybe some time you could go to the planetarium and come to my house after. If you can't remember who I am, remember the fish? Well, this is certainly the worst Christmas ever. I hope yours is better. Maybe I'll see you again next summer. Your friend, Robert.*

"I want a cookie," I say and add loyally, "Stupid Christmas."

I fall asleep on the couch then and have a half-dream, half-memory of the time Grandpa took me to the planetarium, just him and me. It was only last year, when he could still drive the car and remember the names of things and teach me about the stars. We sat in the chairs that tipped way back and held hands while the lights went out, and then Grandpa said, "Open your eyes, Albert, this is the best part." I opened my eyes and saw the stars come on one by one, until thousands of tiny lights prickled against the black velvet of the night sky. A man's deep voice came on over the loudspeaker to explain how the ancients believed that stars were the souls of people who had died and gone to the next world. Grandpa held my hand through the whole show, even after I stopped being afraid.

Dancing with Mean Megan

The phone rings in the middle of the night, and after a few minutes it rings again. Dad, who is dreaming of sitting in a deck chair with a newspaper while Dexter and I shriek and laugh together down by the lake, hears it and wakes. Mom, who is dreaming of the house she grew up in, in St. John's, and the smell of pumpkin pie, hears it and thinks, It's a wrong number, let the answering machine get it. Dexter, who is dreaming a complicated whirling dream with colors and flavors and smells, all pink and purple and fruity, with sparkly clothes and music and dancing, hears it and moans and rolls over and tries to burrow back into her dream. I, who have been dreaming comfortable Edie dreams of dark rainy afternoons at home with books and cats and cheese sandwiches, hear it faintest of all and am asleep again before I even know I've woken.

Only Dad gets out of bed.

At the breakfast table, Dexter sits alone. She's set two places. When I sit at my chair, she coaxes a crumpet from the toaster with a fork and puts it on my plate.

"OH MY GOD," I say, rubbing my eyes. "You're making my breakfast."

"I'm in charge," Dexter says.

Normally I would dispute this kind of claim loudly and lengthily, appealing to Mom, and Dad too if he hadn't already left for work. But there's an eerie quiet to the house this morning, and Dexter has not automatically told me to shut up, which is bizarre. She also looks tired, more tired than her normal just-rolled-out-of-bed tired, and her mouth is a bit raisiny, like Mom's gets when she's worried or annoyed.

"Where's Mom?" I ask.

"They had to go to the hospital," Dexter says. "We have to get ourselves ready for school."

I look up at the kitchen clock, at the big slice of pie the hands make—quarter to eight—and the second hand sweeping so slowly you have time to think about every single second and the eternity of space in between.

Mom sits at the kitchen table. Her face is white with tiredness, but her voice is still the same. When I got home from school and saw her face, I was afraid everything might somehow have changed.

"Grandpa's stable," Mom says. "That means he's not getting any worse. Grandma is with him now."

Mom and I are alone in the kitchen, sitting on the bench in the kitchen nook; my car pool got home before Dexter's. I snuggle right up against Mom and hook my arm through hers.

"How was school?" Mom says, so I tell her about this month's volunteer time: helping the grade twos make Valentines with red construction paper and fat colored markers and scissors and glitter glue.

"You could make a special get-well Valentine for Grandpa," Mom says. That's what I'm doing when Dexter gets home and Mom goes into her bedroom with her to tell her the news about Grandpa, closing the door behind her because there's no need to distract me from my project, Mom says.

Dexter is crying. Her eyes and nose are red and her shoulders are shaking, but she doesn't make any sound. "Ssh," Mom says, over and over. We're sitting in the kitchen all together now. Dexter burst out of her bedroom and ran to the bathroom, startling me. She slammed the door behind her and blew her nose and flushed the toilet about a hundred times while Mom stood outside, talking to her in a low voice. When she came out, Mom led her into the kitchen and sat her down on the bench next to me. Mom put milk in a pan on the stove for hot chocolate while Dexter snuffled and shivered and tried to calm down. I feel my own face trying to cry too, even though my brain doesn't want to. Wordlessly I pass my sister my last uncut piece of red construction paper and some other supplies, and after a minute Dexter folds the piece into smaller and smaller squares and starts to chop at it with her scissors. I'm about to complain to Mom that I was just trying to be nice and Dexter is ruining my very last piece of good paper when I realize she's treating her Valentine heart like a snowflake, cutting tiny decorations into the folds. When she opens it out she'll have something very beautiful and lacy and perfect and terribly, terribly fragile.

"Please," Dexter says.

    "Please," I say.

"Help me, Jamie," Mom says to Dad in the private adult voice that excludes Dex and me even though we're all in the same room.

"It's all right," Dad says to her in the same voice, and then in his normal voice he says, "Mom doesn't want the two of you to get upset. But I know Grandma and Grandpa would both like to see you very much. Only you have to remember it's only for a very short visit because Grandpa gets tired very quickly. He won't be able to talk to you but he'll know you're there, and that will make him feel much better. But you have to be on your best behavior in the hospital. No fighting with each other or loud voices or bouncing around."

"I never bounce around!" I say indignantly, because he's looking especially at me for this last part.

"Get your coats then, quickly," Mom says, and Dexter and I rush to get our coats and shoes while our parents, already dressed to go out, wait by the front door. Dad has the car keys in his hand, and Mom has our homemade Valentines in one of the big mustard-yellow envelopes Dad uses for work.

Grandpa lies in a room that has three other beds. Two of them are empty; the third one has a curtain like a shower curtain drawn all the way around it so we can't see who's inside. Grandpa has a needle attached to a plastic tube taped to his arm, and he wears pale blue hospital pajamas with short sleeves that stick out from his shoulders like awkward little wings. The skin on his face looks like clay someone has pushed all out of place. His mouth won't close, and he looks angry. His eyes follow us, but he doesn't talk. The only noise he makes is when Dad shows him our Valentines and then puts them on the bedside table, where Grandpa can't see them. He makes a moaning noise and jerks his head until Dad puts the cards on his chest, tucked under the arm without the tube, and then he quietens down again.

Grandma thanks us for the lovely cards; she says she knows that's what Grandpa is thinking. Dad tries to persuade her to go down to the cafeteria to get a coffee and a sandwich, but she won't go. In the end, Dad goes down himself and comes back with the coffee in a paper cup and the sandwich in cardboard and cling-wrap and sets them by Grandma's chair. They're still sitting there when visiting hours end and it's time for us to leave.

"Tae kwon do?" Mom asks, her pen poised over the rec center catalog. "Beading?" Dexter and I are picking our spring activities. Or, rather, I'm picking while Dexter sits with us doing her math homework, since Dexter always chooses the same activity: Advanced Ballet.

I shake my head and look at the window. Valentine's Day is over and Easter is still far, far away. Grandpa is still in hospital, but he's too sick for any visitors except for Grandma and Dad, who goes every evening after work and comes home after my bedtime. Rain runs down the windows, making blurred swoops on the glass. Beyond the window the sky is gray and the trees waver like kelp in an aquarium.

"Poetry?" Mom turns a page. "Yoga? Popcorn Crafts and Fun?"

"Dance," I say.

Mom's and Dexter's heads snap up like they're puppets whose head-strings have been jerked.

"What?" Mom says, which is so unusual she even corrects herself. "Pardon?"

"Dance," I say.

"You hate dance," Dexter says.

"You tried once, remember?" Mom says more gently. "With Madame Elenskaya? You didn't like it at all."

This is true. I tried Beginner Ballet about half a million years ago, when I was five and really wanted a pink tulle skirt like Dexter's. I went through a phase, believe it or not, of wanting to be like Dex in every way. But there was no tutu in Beginner Ballet, only gym clothes, shorts and T-shirts, and bare feet. I thought the barre was a monkey bar, which didn't endear me to Madame Elenskaya. We had a further difference of opinion about exactly how many times a person should be made to do second position before she was good enough to move on to third. So I dropped out after a couple of weeks, and my fascination with all things Dex waned from that moment.

"Dance," I say.

"Not ballet," Dexter says urgently, speaking only to Mom now. "Please, Mom, not ballet. She'll embarrass me."

"What kind of dance?" Mom says.

I don't know.

"Mommy!" Dexter yells. "You're not listening to me!" She's almost in tears.

"You can't choose!" I yell suddenly. "It's my spring activity!" I feel close to tears also. We stare at each other, startled and confused. Tears come quickly these days.

"Maybe, Dexter," Mom says, gently stroking Dexter's hair back from her forehead to calm her down, "you could recommend a dance class you think Edie might like. Since you're the dance expert in the family." She says this in a straightforward way, almost like she's talking to another adult instead of to her daughter. I find this infuriating, but also intriguing. Why should it be Dexter's choice? What will Dexter choose?

Dexter takes the rec center catalog and starts turning the pages. She bites her lip. She reads one page for a while and then turns it and starts to read the next one. She's frowning, but it's a concentration frown instead of a frustration frown.

"This one," she says finally, holding the catalog so I can't see and pointing something out to Mom.

"What is it?" I ask while Mom reads the page, nodding slowly.

"Flamenco," Dexter says. "You get to stamp your feet."

"Flamenco," Mom says slowly, trying out the idea.

"Flamenco," I say. I have no idea what that is. It sounds perfect.

"No smile," the instructor says. "Little girl. No smile."

The girl next to me, who's been whispering and tittering with the girl on her other side, stops abruptly.

"First, I show," the instructor says. "Little girls watch."

The instructor, whose name is Senora Ruiz, presses a button on the CD player that sits on a chair at the front of the room. Nothing happens.

"Ah!" Senora Ruiz says, looking peeved. I wonder if she'll have to cancel the class now that there's no music.

I remember once at Madame Elenskaya's when the elderly man who played the piano started to cough only ten minutes into the class. At first he coughed delicately, his fingers still poised over the keyboard, and then he coughed harder, his hand over his mouth, and finally he turned away and hacked into a handkerchief, leaning far over the side of the bench, while we all fidgeted and looked at Madame Elenskaya. Finally the old man got up and left the room, still coughing, and Madame Elenskaya followed him, and when she came back she told everyone to put their street clothes and shoes on because class was over for that day. I assumed that was because there was no music for us to dance to. At the next class the pianist was a serious young girl with funky glasses and a long brown turtleneck dress, and we never saw the old man again. I think of the other bed in Grandpa's hospital room, the one with the shower curtain all the way around it, and can't shake the idea that the old man is there.

Senora Ruiz, though, does not appear fazed by the failure of her CD player. She points to a tall girl in the front row and says, "With me." She starts to clap, and the girl claps along with her. "Yes," Senora Ruiz says, and the girl continues clapping on her own, slow and steady, as she's been shown. When one or two other students start to clap too, Senora Ruiz shushes them impatiently, waving them off with her hands like they're flies buzzing over her salad. I decide I'm a little bit afraid of Senora Ruiz.

The tall girl claps; the class watches. Senora Ruiz stands very tall at the front of the room and suddenly stamps her foot. Everyone flinches. The clapping continues, and Senora Ruiz slowly raises her arms over her head and begins doing something complicated with her wrists and fingers, weaving and winding them in tricky patterns, like she's pulling invisible threads out of the air. Slowly, while her hands continue to work, she brings her arms back down to her waist, and then she stamps again and begins to dance in time to the lonely clapping. With one hand she snags up her long skirt so we can see her feet, in uncomfortable-looking black boots, as they tap and stamp and make patterns. What fascinates me even more, though, is her face. Sure enough, she doesn't smile. She frowns as though she's concentrating very hard on hearing a sound that's very faint and very far away. Her eyebrows knit intently, and her eyes seem to go more black. You could say she seems angry, but that's not quite the right word. My own face makes a mirror of Senora Ruiz's, the intense frown of someone trying very hard to understand something just out of reach. It feels so much like the way I've been feeling lately that I find when the dance is over I haven't erased the look from my own face, and Senora Ruiz is staring straight at me.

"Little girl, very good," Senora Ruiz says. She sounds surprised.

Practicing. I practice all over the house, but particularly in my room, in the kitchen and in the bathroom, where the floor has no carpet and the echo makes my stamping sound especially forceful. Mom, surprisingly, doesn't mind me practicing in the bathroom; she thinks I'm studying myself in the mirror and Polishing My Technique. Nothing is further from the truth. Though my eyes are open, I'm like a sleepwalker when I dance; I am aware of very little. I dance by the feel of it: the stomp of my feet, the click of my fingers, the sway of my hips. I only have to imagine that lonely clapping and I can step into the dance like stepping onto a train and be carried away out of myself.

The clapping and stamping are not as comprehensible to Dex, who claims I'm doing it just as an Edie-thing, to annoy her personally. Mom points out that it was Dexter who chose that particular class for me, because of the stamping, and now she will just have to Live With The Consequences Of Her Decision. Ordinarily this would be quite satisfying, but lately I'm more and more distracted and only want to get back inside myself, into the place where there's nothing other than the rhythm in my body.

More distressingly, Dad doesn't seem to appreciate my new passion and more than once asks me if I would mind dancing more quietly because he has a headache. He often has a headache lately. Once, when I was practicing fairly quietly (I thought) in my room, he stormed upstairs and snapped at me to stop. I started to cry, and he hugged me and called me his pumpkin and apologized for being short-tempered and said he was just worried about some things, that was all. Finally Mom comes up with the solution, which is to send me to dance down in the laundry room, on the cold concrete floor, where I won't be stomping over anyone's head or getting in anyone's way. Mom offers to bring my sister's big body-length mirror down to the room, igniting major protest from Dex. But I tell her I like to dance with my eyes closed; it's not strictly true, but it doesn't really feel like a lie. Once, when Mom comes down and interrupts me by accident with a basket of laundry, she finds me winding my hands over my head with the lights off, in almost complete darkness.

"Why dancing, Edie?" Mom asks me one night a couple of weeks later as she's tucking me into bed. I can't explain that it's because of Grandpa in his hospital bed, unable to move, and the machine that beeped so quietly and steadily behind him, as lonely as the sound of one single, frightened girl clapping just exactly the way she's been shown.

Value Village is an Edie store, not a Dexter store. It's not pretty or trendy or expensive. You don't often bump into your school friends there so that you can all rush into the change rooms and try on the exact same shirt or skirt at the same time and all come out posing like models in a magazine, or girls in a movie, with your arms in the air and your hips cocked, saying Ta-da! for your mothers. (I saw this once with my own eyes and told Mom at the time, discreetly I thought, that it made me want to puke. The other mothers smiled, but I wasn't given any dessert that night for using a rude word about my sister.) No, Value Village is fluorescent lights high, high up on the dirty ceiling, and tables of pots and pans with burnt-on crusts that can't be removed, and chipped plates and mismatched cutlery, forks with bent tines, spoons without shine, dull knives. Value Village is shelves of used books with broken spines and covers curved double and children's books I'm not allowed to touch because they're warped by food and drool. Value Village is lonely-eyed men and women picking through racks bulging with used clothes that have been sorted by color into rainbows of uselessness: acid-washed blue jeans, fluorescent orange T-shirts, tie-dyed purple vests, cracked and scaly red vinyl jackets that once passed for leather, tea-green sateen ball gowns with sweat stains under the arms and loose threads where the beading has torn away. The change rooms have dust bunnies the size of real bunnies on the floor and no mirror, so that you have to step out in front of everyone in whatever you're wearing. The cashiers all seem sleepy and depressed. But Value Village is where I found my Arabian Nights sandals with the gold straps and the rhinestones and the upcurled toes, and my dark green cape with only a tiny moth hole near the collar, and my floppy velvet Shakespeare hat with the matching feather, and my blousy white pirate shirt from two Halloweens ago.

Value Village is where Mom and I go to find a skirt for Senora Ruiz's flamenco class, because Senora Ruiz says you can't dance flamenco in gym shorts and bare feet; whoever comes to the next class without leather-soled shoes and a long skirt won't be allowed to take part. I have patent leather Mary Janes with leather soles that make the right *click-slap-stamp* sounds on the concrete in the laundry room, but I don't own one single skirt, and Dex's are all too big, even if she were willing to loan me one, which is highly, extremely, utterly doubtful in any case.

"This is nice," Mom says, pulling out a flippy, deeply pleated, red and white cheerleader's skirt that would barely reach my knees. I say, "OH MY GOD," and shove the skirt back into the maw of the rack before anyone might see. "Longer," I say, trying to make up for this meanness, because Mom hasn't sat in on one of my classes yet and can't be expected to understand that this particular skirt is all wrong. I want a skirt that frowns like Senora Ruiz, not angrily, but darkly and seriously. I will know it when I see it.

"Longer," Mom repeats thoughtfully. Next she pulls out a long skirt in a crinkly fabric with a busy blue and ivory Indian pattern. This skirt is momentarily distracting because it reminds me of the hippie girls on the island last summer, and I can tell Mom likes it too. "This must be from the seventies," Mom says, which I know was the time when Mom was a young girl and probably wore clothes like this. I've seen old photographs of Mom before she knew Dad, when she had long, straight hair parted in the middle and wore embroidered blouses and long skirts sort of like this one. But it's still not quite right, and I have to shake my head. Mom strokes the skirt once or twice and puts it back on the rack.

The search is slow and tedious, and nothing seems right. I get discouraged. While Mom continues to sort through the racks, occasionally pulling out some inappropriate item and holding it up for my dark, serious frown, I drift farther and farther away. I become interested in the conversation of a couple of teenage girls, older than Dex, whose pale faces look even paler in contrast to their dyed black hair and black lipstick and head-to-toe black clothes. I know from Dex that these girls are called Goth, which is more a city-girl than a Coquitlam-girl thing. Dex, I know, has no time for Goth. They, and a few other subcategories of the terminally weird (as Dex refers to them), are about the only teenagers you ever see in Value Village.

"This," one of the Goth girls says to the other, holding up a black T-shirt with the word *succubus* across the chest in ornate white script. I don't know this word.

"These," the other Goth girl replies, holding up a pair of heavy brass candlesticks splotched with verdigris, which is a word I know and love. It means the greeny blue sheen old brass gets when it hasn't been cleaned in a long time.

"Edie," Mom calls, and I look up to see her waving a blue taffeta skirt with a crinoline that sticks out about three feet on each side. "It's long!" Mom calls. I shake my head, No!

The girls smile at each other and at me, pityingly.

"Shopping with your mom is such a drag," one of them says.

"Ew, don't even talk to her," the other says.

"This is *cool*," the first one says, stressing the word in a way that suggests she's using my vocabulary, not her own, because she's too, too cool to use a word like cool. The skirt she holds up is long and black and plain, with a long slash up one leg showing a blood-colored lining. At the top of the slash is stitched a black fabric rose.

"Aw!" the second girl says jealously, having already forgotten me. "I get to try it on after you."

To my surprise, the first girl doesn't head for the change room but simply pulls the waistband wide and steps into it, over the long black skirt she's already wearing. She can't get it over her hips.

"Too small," she says, and the other girl eagerly tries the same move and gets stuck at the same place. They toss the skirt over top of the rack, not bothering to put it back on its hanger, and move on. The first girl glances back at me and says, "Good luck," in a small shy voice that's probably her real voice when she's not being a tough scary Goth.

"Ew!" the second girl says again, and they link arms and go away, laughing loudly.

I snatch the skirt off the rack and pull it on right there in the aisle, over top of my jeans, just as the Goth girls did. It fits. I snag up the hem of the skirt, bunching the material up all along the slash and pinning it with my hand where the rose is so that the blood color shows through the black, and stamp my feet a few times. I know Mom will hate it, and that makes me frown. I'll offer to pay for it from my own money and maybe, just maybe, Mom will understand that this is very, very important. Frowning intensely, still holding the long skirt up in one hand, I walk back to Mom, planning the words I'll say. But Mom takes one look at my face and says, "Is that it?"

I stamp my feet, still frowning.

"I guess that's it," Mom says and doesn't even make me take it off when we go up to the counter to pay.

At my next class, I anxiously examine the other girls' skirts—long and short, patterned and plain, some obviously resurrected from the dress-up bag (a black skirt from a witch costume with a fluorescent yellowish white spider ironed on the side) or the back of the closet (a private school kilt)—but I see none I prefer to my own. I seek Senora Ruiz's glance, hoping for another private gesture of approval, just between the two of us, but her eyes merely pass over her class with faintly glazed distaste. Two girls in running shoes are sent to sit out the class on a bench by the side wall, which is all mirrors. The smaller one snivels a little, but Senora Ruiz shoots her a stern look and she immediately goes quiet. The other one glumly rubs her sneakered toe into the hardwood dance floor until it squeaks, and then Senora Ruiz gives her a look too; after that she sits very still.

"How was it?" Mom asks as we wait together in the rec center lobby for Dexter's Advanced Ballet class to let out.

"Exceptional," I say.

Mom looks at her watch and sighs. In theory our classes end at the same time, one of the reasons she's so pleased I'm enjoying myself—it makes the driving that much easier. But Dexter can't be rushed, particularly through the removal of her pink ballet shoes, with their long silk ribbons and stained points where her toes have bled.

When Dexter finally comes out, wearing a gray hooded track suit over her leotard, Mom says, "Where's Megan?" Usually we give Mean Megan a ride home on Saturdays, which is bad because it means spending time with Mean Megan, but good because it guarantees me the front seat so the older girls can whisper and giggle together in the back.

"She doesn't take ballet anymore," Dex says. "She switched to jazz and hip-hop." She says this so carefully, so neutrally, I know they must have had a raging argument about it and perhaps aren't even friends anymore.

At supper, I practice my steps under the table until Dexter kicks me to make me stop.

"Mom!" I say.

"Mom!" Dexter says.

The phone rings. Dad answers. He listens for a moment, starts to say something, then screws his eyes up tight and stays that way for three, four, five breaths. His shoulders shake once, and then he turns his back to us.

"Girls," Mom says, "I want you to take your suppers and go finish in front of the TV."

We do as we're told, chewing slowly and staring at the TV's dull black eye, which neither of us has made a move to turn on.

Grandpa's funeral is a week later. First will be the church service; then there will be an afternoon and evening at Grandma and Grandpa's house—now just

Grandma's house—that Dad calls a "reception" and
Mom calls a "wake." They decide that Dexter and I can't
come to either the church or the house because we're
too young and will get too upset. The night Grandpa
died, Dad went out and brought Grandma home with
him so she wouldn't have to spend that first night alone.
We cried with her then. The funeral and what comes
after, Mom explains, are for people who knew Grandpa
but weren't as close to him as his own two favorite girls.
At the last minute, though, Dex throws a fit, crying and
begging to go with them to say good-bye to Grandpa.
I, who have cried so much in the past few days I feel
scoured out, am unable to produce one tear more.
I watch numbly while our parents struggle to calm the
now near-hysterical Dex.

"Sweetie," Mom says. "But your friend is here." And
that's true: Mean Megan has come over to keep Dex
company this evening. I was allowed to invite my friend
Sam, but at the last minute Sam's mom phoned to say
Sam's little brother had come down with chicken pox
and Sam was in quarantine. I don't really mind. I don't
especially want to watch funny videos or play Boggle
and pretend to have a good time. With Mean Megan
taking care of Dex, I can just read or, more accurately,
stare at the white space between the words while my
mind roams far far away.

Mom is talking very softly to Dexter now, but I hear my own name in the flow of words. I understand she's telling Dex that I can't come along but I can't be left alone.

"That's okay, Mrs. Snow," Mean Megan says suddenly. "I have my St. John's Ambulance."

We look at her blankly.

"My babysitting certificate," Mean Megan says. "I can do CPR."

Then Dex is getting her good black shoes and her good black felt coat with the buckles and nobody is exactly telling her not to. I realize my sister was already wearing a dark skirt and sweater and has probably been planning this—grim determination collapsing into panic—since she got up this morning.

"Mommy," I say, meaning to protest, but no one hears. Mom is now having a quiet word with Mean Megan, both of them glancing meaningfully at me from time to time.

"Daddy," I say, but he only gives me a hug and says I'm his pumpkin and his princess and they'll all be home very, very soon, which I know—it's not even lunchtime yet—is not close to being true. Then they're gone, and the door is closed, and Mean Megan and I are left staring at each other in the front hall. I think I might have a few tears left after all.

I'm remembering everything I've ever tried to forget about Mean Megan, everything that's making me think this day can't get too much worse. Remembering, for instance, the time Mean Megan invited me to play hide-and-seek with her and Dexter and, while I hid, persuaded Dexter it was all right to abandon the game and go look at magazines in Dexter's room. They left me squooshed under the kitchen sink for close to half an hour, so that I couldn't stand straight and my foot felt like needles when Mom finally opened the cupboard door to throw away a handful of carrot scrapings, and I scared her Half Out Of Her Wits. Remembering, also, the time right after Mean Megan and Dexter became friends—this was a few years ago—when we were all in the same school together, and I was really quite small and didn't know any better and tried to say hi to Mean Megan in the hallway, and Mean Megan ignored me and walked on by. Reflecting, too, that Mean Megan is as proud of her own prettiness as Narcissus (I know about him from my book on the ancient Greeks) and once looked at Dexter's and my baby pictures on the windowsill in the living room and pointed out that I was not nearly as cute anymore and would only get uglier until the day I died.

"I'm really sorry about your grandpa," Mean Megan says.

No! No! That's worse! Niceness is worse!

"I have to go to the bathroom," I say as I run there and slam the door just the way Dexter is doing so often lately, so Mean Megan won't see me cry. I stay in the bathroom until the crying stops. It's interesting how my mind and my crying often seem to part ways. My eyes will be running and my nose sniffling and my shoulders shaking even after my mind has calmed down and is not feeling quite, quite so terribly bad and is even starting to think about other things. Hopefully by now Mean Megan will have gone to watch TV in the den. I flush the toilet and wash my hands and brush my teeth, for no particular reason, and splash cold water on my eyes, pat them dry and open the door. Mean Megan is sitting on the floor opposite the bathroom door, leaning against the wall, finger-combing long strands of her straight black hair.

"Are you okay?" she says, flipping her hair back and looking closely at me.

"What's CPR?" I say.

"Say I make you lunch," Mean Megan says. "Say you start to choke on your sandwich. I could save your life."

I see her get dreamy and I know that in her mind she's saving my life and telling my parents all about it when they get home and getting a medal for bravery.

"I could save my own life," I say. "I could spit the sandwich out, duh."

"Say you were in a swimming pool," Mean Megan says.

I can see where this conversation is going. I stomp past her down the hall to the kitchen. Mean Megan follows me.

"Say you swallowed some water and were choking," she says. "Say you stopped breathing. I could give you artificial respiration and bring you back to life."

"Stop it," I say.

"I also know what to do about cuts, poison, dizziness, faintness, abrasions, fever, insect bites, allergic reactions and vomiting," Mean Megan says. "I can apply a tourniquet. Want to play a game?"

"No!" I say. I get a plate and a glass down from the cupboard. After a second, I make myself say, "Do you want a sandwich?"

"What kind?"

I'm about to break one of Mom's food rules and can't say the word out loud. Instead, I go to the fridge, pull out the jar of chocolate spread and hold it up for Mean Megan to see. Mean Megan frowns and nods.

"You can't tell," I say. Chocolate spread is strictly a Weekend Food.

"Neither can you," Mean Megan says. "I'm not allowed to have chocolate."

"What?" I say.

"Chocolate ruins the complexion, my mother says."

I make two sandwiches bulging with glossy chocolate spread and slap the plates down on the table. I feel like the eighteenth-century gentleman from another of my books who slaps down his gloves when he's annoyed with someone, as a challenge. Throwing down the gauntlet this is called. A gauntlet is a glove.

Mean Megan eats her sandwich and says it's good.

"What kind of game?" I ask suspiciously.

"You lie down," Mean Megan says, "and pretend to be choking. And I'll save your life."

"No," I say.

"I could do your hair."

"No!" I say.

"Pretend you have a broken arm? Paint your nails?"

"Stop it!" I say.

"I know," Mean Megan says. "I can teach you to dance."

"This is ridiculous," I say. "I know how to dance. I have my own class now."

"Since when?" Mean Megan demands. "You suck at dance. I'm sorry, but this is true."

This is the kind of "I'm sorry" that means its own opposite. "Dexter didn't tell you about my class?"

Mean Megan shakes her head. "Ever since I quit ballet, she won't talk to me anymore."

"Is that why you're being nice to me?"

Mean Megan nods.

"She's not here," I say. "She won't notice." Which is true but pretty nasty. I feel bad as soon as I say it. So I add, "Dexter wouldn't care anyway if you were nice to me."

"That's true," Mean Megan says.

We go into the den and I turn on the TV. I flip the channels with the clicker until I get to the music video channel.

"Cool," Mean Megan says.

I put the clicker down and climb up into the big recliner, the one Grandpa used to like to sit in when he came to visit. I wonder why I'm being nice to Mean Megan.

For a long time we don't talk. Mean Megan watches the TV with a kind of rapt earnest attention, mouthing the lyrics to the songs she knows and leaning forward to study the singing and the dancing and the clothes. She's as crazy as Dexter. I pick out an architecture magazine of Mom's from the pile next to the recliner and look at pictures of beautiful homes around the world. Mean Megan gets up and leaves the room. I hear her go down the hall to the bathroom and then come back via the kitchen. I hear the suck and sigh of the fridge door being opened and the heavy thump of the oven door. I hear the *beepa-beepa-beep* of the timer and I wonder what Mean Megan is doing.

"Your mom told me to put in the leftover lasagna at three-fifty for half an hour for dinner." She sits down on the sofa again and speaks with her eyes riveted to the TV, where a young girl is singing with her head thrown back, at the top of her lungs, in a rainstorm. In the video her clothes are getting soaked, and every time she flicks her hair, droplets fling away like sparks. "I love lasagna," Mean Megan says, watching the girl intently. "I only get it when I come to your house. We don't eat cheese at home."

"That is insane," I say. I've been staring for a long time at a picture of an underground house built into the side of a hill. The house itself is practically invisible, except for the front door.

"My dad is lactose intolerant," Mean Megan says.

We eat our lasagna in front of the TV. Dusty wanders through the room and I instinctively reach to scoop her up but Mean Megan gets there first and holds Dusty in her lap, cooing and petting until Dusty is purring like a vacuum cleaner. "I love your cat, he's so cute," Mean Megan says, finally letting Dusty spill to the ground so she can keep eating her lasagna.

I think my eyes will fall out of my head and roll away across the floor like marbles. "Aren't you allergic?"

"I love cats," Mean Megan says. "They just make me a little sneezy. Or if I, like, forget to wash my hands and touch my eye, my eye will water a little. It's not so bad."

When *Eighties Hour* comes on, Mean Megan asks politely if I would mind if she flipped around, and I politely say she should go ahead. She's given me a particularly cheesy, crusty portion of lasagna, and I'm starting to feel mellow. Eventually she settles on a teen movie about a girl who really, really, really wants to be a ballet dancer even though everyone tells her she's too big and tall. She starts to go on diets until everyone tells her she's too thin, and then she goes to the school doctor and switches to choreography. She starts eating again and gets a date with the school quarterback and is named Prom Queen and makes a courageous teary speech about loving yourself.

"That's your sister," Mean Megan says. "Except her body is perfect just the way it is. She's the best dancer in her class. She wins everything. It's all she ever thinks about, ballet, ballet, ballet."

"I'm Dexter," I say, jumping up from my chair and going *en pointe*, which means on my tippy-toes. "May I have some more lasagna, please?" I ask in a fluting voice with a vague English accent. I do a pirouette. Mean Megan laughs and says, in a pretty good imitation of Dexter's voice,

"You're doing that *wrong*. I'll show you. Watch me. I can do it perfectly. You can't. Nobody is perfect but me."

I don't laugh. I'm watching Mean Megan's face.

"It's true," Mean Megan says, back in her own voice again, shrugging. "She *is* perfect. She's so, so good and I'm just not. I got so sick of it. I just wanted to try something else for a change, something I could do better than her."

"Jazz," I say.

"Hip-hop." Mean Megan flips back to the music video channel and says, "Perfect." A young man is half singing, half talking his way through a song while some pretty girls chirp along in the background. The young man looks annoyed and makes a lot of rapid hand gestures. Mean Megan begins to dance in a loose, relaxed way that I know instantly is very, very cool. When she's finished, I clap.

"Your turn," Mean Megan says.

I push the mute button on the clicker and start to clap slowly and steadily. "With me," I tell Mean Megan. We clap together. "Yes," I say and stop clapping, letting Mean Megan continue on her own. I close my eyes and stamp my feet and lift my hands high over my head and start to dance.

"Show me how to do that," Mean Megan says when I'm done.

We're dancing while my family says good-bye to the last of the guests at Grandma's house and clears away the dirty dishes and mounds of leftover food and does the dishes. We're dancing while my family kisses and hugs Grandma, who says she's fine on her own and doesn't need to borrow our guest room again. We're dancing while my family drives home along cold dark streets, not talking, each in his or her own sealed bubble of tired sadness. We're dancing when my family parks the car in the garage and unbuckles their seat belts and slowly, sadly gets out of the car. We're dancing when my family comes quietly through the front door, in case we're asleep, and follows the sound of laughing and foot stomping to the den. Mean Megan and I have pushed the furniture back and are dancing with our eyes closed. The TV shows a man with long blond hair whapping a guitar against a tree because it's *All-Metal Power Hour*, but we've left the mute on and haven't noticed.

"What are you *doing*?" Dexter asks.

We're hot and red-faced and breathless, and when we see Dexter we both start to laugh.

"You too, Dexter," Mean Megan says. "You have to dance too."

I say, "Dex too."

Maybe Dexter is too stunned to say no, because she starts making her pretty swan movements while I snap my fingers and stomp my feet and Megan grooves and swerves her head around and makes her hip-hop moves. Mom and Dad stand in the doorway of the den, watching us and saying nothing.

A few miles away, Grandma hangs up her clothes and puts on her dressing gown and brushes her hair and cleans her teeth and checks the front door and the back door. Then she slowly goes upstairs to the bedroom she shared with Grandpa, where she lies in bed and speaks to him for a long time before she closes her eyes and makes herself lie still, alone in the big bed, waiting and waiting for sleep.

Dexter in a Whack of Trouble

Up in my attic room, I suddenly cock my head to one side and begin to shake it, like a swimmer trying to get water out of her ear. I've been tracing bugs. This is a slightly unusual Edie activity, but Grandma recently gave me a book called *Insects of the World*, full of excellent words like "mandible" and "thorax," that so bothers Dex she won't be in the same room with it. I've been giving an Egyptian scarab beetle the blackest, shiniest possible carapace (carapace!), experimenting with a combination of black pencil and black crayon, layering them on top of each other and pressing very hard, snapping the tip on the pencil again and again and wearing the crayon's sharp nose down to a blunt snout. Then I felt the tickle deep in my left ear, very slightly annoying. It could be a drop of water left over from my pre-bedtime bath, when I ducked my head under because I was a coelacanth, very bug-eyed and ancient. I start whacking at my head with the heel of my hand to dislodge it.

After a few minutes of this, I go downstairs to get a Q-tip and bump into Dexter in the hall. Dexter is obviously heading for the bathroom too, so I'm forced to make a dash for it, which Dexter thwarts by grabbing at my hair, which I counter by stamping on her foot. An all-out brawl is only averted by the appearance of Mom at the top of the stairs with a laundry basket full of Dad's clean but wrinkled shirts.

"Megan phoned for you earlier," Mom says to Dexter. "I told her you would talk to her at school tomorrow."

"Ha, ha," I say.

Dexter lets go of my hair. "Why didn't you just come get me?"

"You were doing your homework."

"If you were downstairs doing laundry," Dexter says, "and somebody phoned for you, I would get you. I wouldn't say, 'She can't come, she's doing laundry.'"

"Don't argue with your mother." Dad squeezes past the three of us and into the bathroom. The lock clicks.

"No!" I whack my ear a few more times and make my eyes go round to demonstrate to Mom the proven futility of this gesture.

"No!" Dexter points after him. He was carrying his newspaper.

"You'll live," Mom says.

"I was going there!" Dexter says.

"Me first!" I say.

"First up, best dressed!" Dad calls from behind the closed door. I hear the rustle as he turns a page of his newspaper.

"I don't know what that means," Dexter says. "I need to brush my teeth. You can hardly accuse me of wasting time in the bathroom. I don't take reading material in there, like some people."

From behind the closed door, Dad starts to hum.

"Mommy," I say. Thumping my own head again has made me dizzy.

"I have a Q-tip and a spare toothbrush," Mom says. "Just let me go get this ironing squared away and I'll find them for you. You can go wait in my bedroom."

"Can I look in your closet?" Dexter asks.

"Yes."

"She can't look in my closet!" Dad calls from behind the closed door. "It's private!" The newspaper rustles again.

Dexter and Mom exchange a look that means, Ignore him, puh-leese.

The appeal of Mom's closet is the square blue garment bag that hangs at the far, far right. It has a peaked top where the hanger pokes out, like a tent top or a pavilion, and falls all the way to the floor, with a zipper running down its full length. Inside are Mom's very best clothes: a skinny black dress with black threads for straps; a long, strapless, dark red dress with a skirt that poufs out all the way to the ground; a green and gold sari; a pair of very plain black wool pants that Mom loves for some reason; and an orange silk blouse, light and frothy as candy floss, that always makes Dad say, "She's turned into a pumpkin!" when she puts it on. I love my dad and can't imagine much about being married, or what kind of person I'll be married to, but I know for certain it won't be someone who accuses me, in my best favorite clothes, of looking like a gourd.

After Dexter has unzipped the bag just enough so that we can take turns reaching in and identifying each special outfit by feel—we know the textures by heart— she takes down the three shoe boxes from the shelf above the garment bag and lays them in a line on the bed. These, too, we know by heart, but Dexter seems to enjoy the little Christmas shiver of opening each box, each time. I sort of understand, the way I sort of understand the appeal of the clothes—this is Dexter's version of playing dress-up—though I have trouble getting as worked up about them as Dexter. The first box holds Mom's plain black pumps with the two-inch heel. These she keeps nicely polished and shaped by stuffing a wad of tissue paper up into the toe whenever she isn't wearing them, which is most of the time. These are the shoes she wears with the black pants and orange blouse, which is her School Concert and/or Dinner At A Nice Restaurant outfit. The next shoe box contains Mom's sandals: open-toed, whippy straps and a high, pencil-thin heel. They look teetery but Mom always manages, even though she only wears them maybe once a year, when she and Dad go to a concert at the Orpheum. I know Dexter covets these shoes particularly. The closest Dex is allowed to high heels at the moment, despite much reasoning, pleading, begging and groveling, is a pair of platform sneakers with the word "angel" written on the side. These are all very well, Dexter says, but not really the same thing at all.

The last box is my favorite and Dexter's too, though she always pretends otherwise. These contain the low-heeled gold sandals that go with the sari. I've never seen Mom wear the sari and don't know for what possible occasion she could have bought it. Mom is always vague on the subject and says she bought it In Another Life. I covet the sari for my dress-up bag but have never even been allowed to try it on.

Dexter puts the shoe boxes back and turns to Mom's dressing table, where she picks up a lipstick.

"Telling," I say.

"My word against yours." Dexter has the cap off and is twisting up the colored part for a quick swipe at her mouth when the door opens and Dad comes in. "There's trouble in River City!" he says, seeing the lipstick in Dexter's hand. She drops it like it's burnt her and then picks it up calmly and puts it back in its place as though she has nothing to feel guilty about.

"I was looking at the color," she says.

"Trouble with a capital T!" He puts the newspaper by the bed and goes out again.

"Ha," I say.

When Mom comes, Dexter asks if she might phone Megan back now.

"I thought you wanted a toothbrush," Mom says.

"Quit changing the subject!" Dexter yells, and then she stomps into her room and slams the door. This is what Mom and Dad call Going Off Like A Firecracker. Dexter often goes off like a firecracker. She can't seem to help it. I suspect she often surprises herself as much as everybody else with her fits of sudden, intense anger directed at nothing and everything.

"Dexter and the telephone, sitting in a tree," I say.

"You should be nicer to your sister." Mom rummages around in her top dresser drawer and pulls out a jar of Q-tips. "You hurt her feelings more often than you know, always laughing at her."

I say, "ARE YOU OUT OF YOUR MIND?"

"I don't know," I hear Mom say to Dad much later, long after I'm supposed to be in bed. I've gotten up to go to the bathroom one last time and hear their voices from the living room. "Every little thing sets her off lately. She's getting so rude. I just don't know what to do with that girl."

Dexter? Perfect Dexter? Princess Dexter?

Mean Megan slumps in Dexter's bedroom doorway like she'll fall over if something doesn't prop her up. "Dave and Celine say I can have a party," she says, as though this is the most boring news on the planet. "After final exams. Girls and—"

Dexter shrieks, making Mean Megan jump. Dexter has just found my drawing of an Egyptian scarab beetle, with a carapace blacker than the night, leafed between the pages of her English binder. I'm able to observe all this from my hiding place in the linen cupboard with the latticework doors. I have an excellent view of Dexter's room from here as long as she leaves her door open. If I get caught, I can simply say I'm looking for the key chain I left in the pocket of my jeans when I threw them in the laundry. I got this idea from seeing Mean Megan casually twirling the key ring that hangs from the big loopy chain on her belt.

"Get it away!" Dexter says.

Mean Megan, who's not so squeamish, takes the beetle paper, crumples it and throws it into Dexter's garbage can.

"—and boys," she finishes.

"Ooh," Dexter says, shaking her hands to rid them of the feel of the big paper bug. "Who are you inviting?"

"I don't know," Mean Megan says. "Practically the whole school, I guess. Dave and Celine say I shouldn't make anyone feel alienated." Mean Megan calls her parents by their first names. She wants Dexter to come over to her house after school every day since her parents don't get home until suppertime or after, but Mom thinks that's too much. She worries about them spending too much time together without adequate supervision, almost certainly ignoring their homework and getting up to who-knows-what. Once a week is quite enough Megan-time, in Mom's opinion.

"You hate Megan," Dexter says.

"I like Megan very much," Mom counters.

"You hate me," Dexter says.

"Don't be a goof," Mom says.

"Don't call me a goof!" Dexter says, and Mom laughs.

"I don't hate anybody," Mom says. "I wouldn't think you'd want to spend every single day with your friend anyway. You two get into enough arguments as it is. You'll enjoy the time you spend together more if you don't have so much of it. Anyway, when would you practice your dance if you spent every day at Megan's?"

"I am a prisoner," Dexter says, and Mom tells her not to be morose.

"Yeah," I say from the back seat. "Morose."

"Shut up, little garbage," Dexter says.

"See, that right there," Mom says. "We don't speak to each other that way in our family."

Mean Megan tends to speak her mind because Dave and Celine say that's healthy. This makes other kids a bit afraid of her: so cool and pretty and quick-tongued. Sweet as vinegar, Dad said once about Mean Megan. But I knew from the afternoon of Grandpa's funeral that Mean Megan envies our family as much as Dexter envies Megan's freedom, and I found myself in the odd position of wanting to defend Megan, though against what I wasn't quite sure.

"Want a tea?" Mean Megan says. She takes a couple of cans out of her knapsack. The cans are pink and green and have Chinese characters on them.

Through the slats, I see Dexter pop her tea and take a sip and try not to make a face while Mean Megan gets out a paper and pen and starts a list of people to invite.

"We're going to need a budget," Mean Megan says after a while. By this time she's lying on her stomach on Dexter's bed, sucking her pen. Dexter is lying on her stomach on the bed facing the other way, listening to music on the headphones because Mean Megan says the radio is distracting her.

"For decorations?" Dexter says, really loudly because of the headphones. Mean Megan gives her the kind of look she usually gives me. Dexter quickly takes the headphones off. "What?" she says.

"Are you in grade three? We're not having decorations," Mean Megan says. "I suppose next you're going to want games. What we need are food and tunes."

"I wasn't," Dexter says.

"Games," Mean Megan says, wrinkling her forehead. "Now that you mention it…"

"I didn't!" Dexter says.

"Games," Mean Megan says to herself and starts writing again.

The next day, in our after-school car pool, Mean Megan tells Dexter that Dave and Celine have agreed to give her two hundred dollars for the party.

"Don't look so stunned," Mean Megan adds. "You're going to have to help me choose chips and pop and stuff—whatever you think people will want to eat. I don't know anything about those kinds of crappy foods."

Mom and I, in the front seat, glance at each other and away, biting the insides of our cheeks. We can tell Mean Megan is very, very happy.

"What date was that again?" Mom says.

Dexter looks like the top of her head is about to blow off, like a volcano. Mom and Dad are laughing at her. She's been talking about nothing but the party for the past week, and they know perfectly well the date is this coming Saturday night, four days away. Now Mom stands with her pen poised over the calendar on the kitchen wall, pretending she doesn't know anything about it, while Dad and I smirk.

"It's Saturday!" Dexter yells. "Don't do that!"

"I'm sorry, sweetie," Mom says right away. "I know you're excited."

"I'm not excited!" Dexter yells.

"There's going to be boys," I whisper to Dad. He makes a face like his eyeballs are about to fall out of their sockets.

"That's disgusting!" he whispers back. I giggle so hard I fall out of my chair.

"Would you all grow up!" Dexter yells.

Fortunately, Mom's not paying too close attention. She's squinting at the calendar and mumbling to herself.

"This Saturday we have a dinner at the Corrigans'," she says. "I forgot you wouldn't be home. I guess we'll just have to find a babysitter for Edie."

I groaned. "Not Mrs. Halibut," I say. "Mrs. Halibut" is our family's secret name for Mrs. Hammett, the old widow who lives down the street, who loves children but has no idea how to care for them. Last time she tried to teach me to crochet and made me drink carrot juice and take cod liver oil. "Can't I stay by myself?"

"During the day, not at night," Mom says. "When you're twelve."

Mom phones Grandma, but Grandma has her book club that night and has already started baking for it. Grandma's baking is epic, and once the machinery is in motion it can't easily be halted.

"Why can't I go to the party?" I ask.

"NO!" Dexter says. "NO, NO, NO, NO, NO!"

I've never been to Mean Megan's house and never wanted to go to Dexter and Mean Megan's stupid party. Nevertheless, I enjoy making Dex go off like a firecracker. I say, "I could stay in a whole other room and watch TV.

I could promise not to come out and bug them. I could take my sleeping bag. I wouldn't be any trouble at all."

Dad looks at Mom, eyebrows raised, as though to say, Why not?

What Dexter calls me next I'm not allowed to repeat. I don't think Dexter really meant to say it aloud. The word just falls out of her mouth onto the floor and sits there like a little black stone. Even Dexter looks shocked.

The silence that comes next is interesting.

Mom drops us off at Mean Megan's house on the afternoon of the party with a stern warning to both of us to behave and get along.

"I know," I say.

"This is ridiculous," Dexter says.

Mom power-locks the car doors.

"Fine!" Dexter says. "I promise or whatever."

"That's better," Mom says and unlocks the doors. We spill out. I've brought so much stuff—games and clothes and books and sleeping bag and pillow and blanket—that Dexter has to help me carry it all. She grabs the sleeping bag, which is tightly rolled, and my knapsack with my books, and leaves me to grapple with the odds and ends.

"You're sure Megan's parents will be there?" Mom says.

"Hi, kids!" a voice calls out. We look up and see Celine leaning out an upstairs window. She's got long black hair and she's really pretty. Mean Megan has told Dexter that she and her mom share each other's clothes. "I'll be down in a minute!" she calls.

"See you at eleven AM," Mom says sweetly to us. Dexter and I will sleep over at Mean Megan's after the party so we can help Mean Megan clean up. That is Dexter's argument for letting us stay over, though I overheard Mean Megan telling Dexter that Dave and Celine have a cleaning lady because they say housework numbs the soul. Cleaning up will be her problem, not ours.

"Fancy," I say, meaning the house. I stand beside Dexter on the front step, waiting for Mean Megan to come to the door. I can see Dexter is dying to tell me to shut up, but she remembers her promise to Mom, who is, not incidentally, still sitting in the idling car with the window rolled down, waiting to see us safely into the house. Finally we hear footsteps, and then Mean Megan opens the door.

"Hey," Dexter says.

"Hey," Mean Megan says.

"I brought Junior Scrabble and Rex the Raccoon," I say.

Mom backs out of the driveway, waves and drives away.

"Shut up," Dexter says.

"Hey, Edie," Mean Megan says. Ever since Dexter and Mom and Dad came home the night of Grandpa's funeral and found us dancing like a pair of crazy people, Mean Megan has been nice to me. Well, nicer, anyway. It's extremely weird and unnatural, and I keep waiting for it to end. Dexter's waiting for it to end too. That I know for sure.

"Okay, kids?" All of a sudden, Celine appears in the hallway with her car keys in her hand, out of breath and not really looking at us. "Running late, babe," she says to Mean Megan. "I promised your dad I'd pick him up from the tennis club. You'll be okay on your own, right?"

"Of course," Mean Megan says.

"Don't wait up," Celine says, and then she's gone. I know this is not what my mom had in mind, and I feel a little guilty. But then Mean Megan offers to give me a tour of the house, which makes me bounce in my shoes. Dexter rolls her eyes. Mean Megan's house was built by an architect hired by Dave and Celine when Mean Megan was a toddler. It has a lot of skylights and brick and wood floors and is open-plan, which means not a lot of inside walls and not a lot of privacy.

You can sit in the study and talk to someone in the kitchen, forty feet away, while in between someone else sits in the sunken living area watching the world's biggest TV. There's a pool in the backyard and an actual cabana with a white sofa and some rattan furniture and a mini-bar where you can sit with a cold drink in summer and feel like a movie star. Mean Megan's room, upstairs, has a TV and a stereo and its own bathroom and a disco ball hanging from the ceiling and a bed about the size of a farmer's field with black linens Mean Megan chose herself. Black! Also, she has an aquarium containing an electric blue fish with impossibly elegant, draping fins. It's some kind of fighting fish that can't share its tank with any other fish because it will have to kill them. The fish is named Sklar.

"Sklar," Dexter says, tapping the tank with her finger. The fish barely moves, just ripples his fins slightly, disdainfully.

"We're going to be kind of busy," Mean Megan says to me. "Think you can look after yourself for a while?"

"Can I watch TV?" I say.

Mean Megan takes me into the enormous living room and shows me how to work the three clickers for the world's biggest TV. I squirrel myself down into the sofa cushions. Soon I'm clicking away with a big jerk of the hand every time I want to change the channel.

"You don't have to press so hard, stupid," Dexter says, but Mean Megan says actually that one has been a little sticky lately and has been giving everyone trouble.

"You are way too nice to my sister," Dexter says so I will hear. I'm used to it.

"Forget her," Mean Megan says. "We have to clean up and get the snacks out and organize the CDs and skim the pool and get dressed."

It's four fifteen; the party starts at seven. "Let's get dressed first," Dexter says.

Mean Megan gives her a look. They go outside to skim the pool. Unable to resist, I trail after them.

"I didn't bring my bathing suit," Dexter says.

Mean Megan takes what looks like a bright blue fishing net at the end of an impossibly long pole and starts dragging it across the surface of the water, skimming up dead leaves and the occasional bug. "After it gets dark, we can turn the underwater lights on," Mean Megan says. "Nobody's bringing their bathing suit. I only asked Dave to fill it because it looks cool."

"I want to help," I say, mesmerized by the big skimmer.

"Go away!" Dexter says.

"No, that's okay," Mean Megan says. "We've got lots to do. And I have a special surprise for Edie, later."

We spend the next hour getting the house ready: setting up the fridge, arguing about the order of the CDs in the pre-programmable CD player, putting chips in bowls and veggies-and-dip on plates. While I vacuum the entrance hall, Mean Megan and Dexter take all my stuff out of the living room and put it somewhere else. Then Mean Megan orders me and Dexter to go watch TV for a few minutes because she's busy doing something secret with a salad bowl and a piece of paper and a pair of scissors and a pen. She won't let us help or even watch. "You'll see," she says mysteriously.

When Mean Megan is done, Dexter shows her the brownies Mom baked for the party, and I wonder if Mean Megan will say anything about her complexion. But Mean Megan only says "Cool" and shows us what Celine bought for a special treat: wasabi peas. I try one and my eyes instantly water. "Pain," I say. "Pain, pain." I start to cough.

Mean Megan, who can't seem to take her eyes off the glossy brownies, says they're an acquired taste, and for a while she, personally, was addicted to them.

I give Dexter a private look, and Dexter, remembering another promise she made Mom, takes me to show me where the bathroom is. When we get back to the kitchen, Megan is snacking in a vague, distracted way from the bag of wasabi peas, but I see that one of the brownies is gone, and there's a smear of chocolate on the corner of her lip.

"You have chocolate," Dexter says, gesturing at her own mouth, and Mean Megan wipes her lip hard with her thumb without meeting Dexter's eye. Dexter keeps her face carefully neutral. "Is it time to get dressed?" she asks, as though that's what they were talking about all along.

I see this is how, for all their arguments, Dexter and Mean Megan stay friends.

In Mean Megan's room, they spend another hour trying on Mean Megan's clothes, and some of Celine's for good measure. Mean Megan's clothes are more mature than Dexter's—"mature" is Mom's word for it—which means shorter and tighter, with no pink or purple, and nothing that says "angel" on it anywhere. In the end, Mean Megan settles on a white shirt, sleeveless gray sweater, black mini-skirt, knee-high black boots and a lot of silver jewelry. Her hair is in a high ponytail. Dexter chooses a sparkly black dress of Celine's, with straps like a bathing suit, crossed at the back. Dexter asks Mean Megan if Celine knows they're borrowing it, and Mean Megan says not exactly, but since it doesn't fit Celine anymore she can't see why she would mind. I know this reasoning isn't entirely sound, but Dexter's infatuation with the dress and herself in the dress overrides good sense, and she allows herself to be persuaded, especially when Mean Megan loans her a pair of black heels that are Mean Megan's own, and surely, therefore, okay.

They go into the bathroom while I try to get Sklar to look at me. After a long time they come out.

"You're wearing makeup," I say. "Mom's going to kill you."

Dexter and Mean Megan exchange a look I should have paid more attention to. I'll remember it later and kick myself.

"You get your surprise now," Mean Megan says to me. "Ready?"

We all go outside to the pool deck, Dexter tripping uncertainly in her heels. I laugh and clap my hands when I see the transformed cabana. While I was vacuuming, Dexter and Mean Megan arranged all my books and stuff inside, as well as my sleeping bag, and even added a big bottle of pop and a plate of food.

"Like it?" Mean Megan asks.

Something in her voice makes me stop laughing. Mean Megan, who's drawn dramatic black lines with Celine's eyeliner to lengthen her eyes and make the rest of her face a shade paler, looks at that moment about a thousand times witchier than she did at Halloween. She gives me a shove so that I stumble into the cabana, closes the door fast and locks it. Immediately I start banging on the door from the inside.

"All right?" I hear Mean Megan ask Dexter.

"Fine," Dexter's voice says, and I know my sister is rejoicing because the niceness has ended and Mean Megan is once again on her side.

There's no actual danger. If there's a fire, for instance, or a flood, I could probably kick through one of the thin wooden walls or even force my way through the window, which is covered with thin wooden slats, like the slats of a blind set permanently on the diagonal. But such destruction I'll save for a true emergency, and for the first part of the evening the cabana is comfortable enough, even cosy. I eat the plate of food and read my books for a while. Then, when I get bored, I discover that by standing on the chaise longue I can see out the wood-slatted window and straight into the back window of the house. For a while I've been hearing the thumping beat of the stereo, and now I can dimly make out the figures of dancers. I try to dance along, but the chaise longue is cushioned and the satisfying clack of my shoe soles hitting the ground is missing. I try to read a little more, but I'm starting to feel anxious. The light is slowly fading from the sky, and even though I have a nice table lamp in the cabana, I'm aware of being outside on my own when everyone else is in the house. Then, after some long minutes of increasing nervousness, two things happen at once: a strange light clicks on outside, sending wavy ripples of light across the inside walls of the cabana, and I hear voices quite close by.

Mean Megan, it turns out, has been as good as her word and invited the entire class, all twenty-seven eighth-graders, regardless of hipness or coolness or squareness or geekiness or any of those usually devastating categorizations. Someone has turned on the underwater lights in the swimming pool, creating a ghostly green blue light that wobbles on the house and the deck and everywhere it touches. I can't see the speakers but can hear them very well and know they must be right behind the cabana. They're mumbling, and it's a very brief conversation.

"I changed my mind," a girl's voice says.

"Okay," a boy says.

There's silence for another minute or two, and then I hear them move out from behind the cabana, to the cheers of the rest of the group, who must be on the other side of the swimming pool, the side I can't see. After a minute another couple goes past. They're much quieter, but for some rustling sounds and giggling. They too emerge after a couple of minutes to whoops and cheers.

Well, this is interesting, I think.

The kids from my sister's class continue to make their way over in pairs. Mean Megan and a boy named Kalil talk the whole time, or rather Kalil does, nervously, while Mean Megan makes occasional uncharacteristic soft, shy noises of assent. It's at this point I remember Mean Megan's secretiveness with the salad bowl and the scissors and realize the game is about kissing or—in this case—not kissing.

When Dexter and Dwayne Chen, my teacher's son, come over, I can't resist. "Dwayne," I say in my eeriest, ghostliest voice. It will be fun to make him think he's being spied on by some otherworldly being.

"There's someone in the cabana," he says, and that's the end of that.

A moment later the door bursts open and Dexter sticks her flushed, sparkly face inside. "Shut up!" she hisses. "Shut up!"

"You locked me in," I say.

Dwayne appears next to Dexter. "It's Edie!" he says, with a big smile. "You locked her in?" he asks Dexter.

"Freedom!" I say, doing a little dance in and out of the doorway just to bug my sister.

"Game over," Mean Megan calls drily from her perch on the diving board.

"No!" another boy says. "It's my turn!"

"Not a chance, Ivan," a girl with a British accent says.

"Saved by a small child," she adds. "I must thank her."

"No!" the boy named Ivan says again. Everyone is laughing now, except one girl who has gone to the edge of the yard and is leaning over some bushes in a suspicious way. Her shoulders heave once or twice, stop, and then heave again. Ivan jumps to his feet and somehow slips and then he's falling, not to concrete but to cold water. He's slipped right into the pool. The other kids start to laugh until they see him flailing his arms and legs and realize he's panicking.

I see a girl throwing up on some bushes, and a clumsy boy fall into the pool and not start to swim, and the rest of the teens sitting around in a daze until three or four of them jump in after the clumsy boy. They drag him over to the shallow end, where he stands retching and coughing and crying and insisting it's his turn next. I see the big bottle being passed from hand to hand and I think, The cabana is not on fire, and yet. And yet.

I find the phone on the counter in the kitchen and dial the Corrigans' number, which Mom wrote on a slip of paper and tucked into my pocket for emergencies. Mr. Corrigan answers.

"It's Edie," I say. "Is my mom there?"

"Edie!" Mr. Corrigan says and starts to sing an Irish song about his Edie, his sweet briar rose, the way he always does when he hears my name.

"IS MY MOM THERE?" I say again.

While I wait for Mom to come to the phone, I wonder if it will be a matter of weeks or months, or maybe the rest of my life, before my sister will speak to me again.

Sweet Revenge

A warm car makes a good place to sleep, even when you have to share the back seat with sleeping bags and the big orange cooler, and the kettle is on your lap, and your sister has spent the last hundred miles pretending you don't exist, and they still make you wear your seat belt. I close my eyes and let my mind wander around the last two weeks, the aftermath of the party. When Mom and Dad showed up, within ten minutes of my call to Mr. Corrigan, Dexter greeted them not with shame or outrage but with a loose, goofy ease that I knew meant she had been drinking from the big vodka bottle too. Dad got her into the car, where she sat with her head against the headrest and her eyes closed, talking vividly about nothing in particular. Mom took me inside and got me to show her where the phone was, and she began the long business of calling everyone's parents. As they arrived, white-faced with worry, Mom met them at the door and explained in an undertone what had happened. Not until the last kid had been collected did Mom turn to deal with Mean Megan.

"Where are your parents tonight?" she asked.

Mean Megan looked around. "Out," she said. "They're out." She seemed stunned.

"I'm going to leave them a note on the counter here," Mom said. "I want you to come stay with us tonight. Can you go get your pajamas and your toothbrush together?"

"Yes, Mrs. Snow," Mean Megan said and went slowly upstairs.

"Go with her, Edie," Mom said, "and come get me if you think she's going to be sick," so I followed Mean Megan upstairs and watched her get a few things together, slowly, slowly, and then sit on her black bed as though she had just run a marathon and couldn't move another inch. I couldn't tell if she had been drinking like the others or was just overwhelmed by the disaster her party had become. I went downstairs.

"What's she doing?" Mom asked.

"Sitting on the bed," I said.

Mom went upstairs and came down a few minutes later, helping Mean Megan, who was leaning her head against Mom's shoulder, looking exhausted. I followed them out to the driveway, where Dad was holding back Dexter's hair while she puked into the bushes. Mom and Dad exchanged a grim look. Dad got Dexter into the back seat again while Mom settled Mean Megan in the front, and then Dad got in and started the engine while Mom squatted in front of me on the driveway.

"Where were you all this time?" she asked, smoothing my hair back from my forehead the way she usually only did with Dexter.

I almost felt guilty telling because I knew Dexter was in enough trouble as it was. But the night had been split open, stripped bare; there could be no half-truths. "Locked in the cabana," I said, and Mom's mouth went so tight it almost disappeared.

"You're sure they didn't give you any drinks?" Mom asked for about the eleventh time, and I said no, I was sure. Then Mom got in the back seat next to Dexter, and I squeezed in next to her and we all went home. I was dimly aware of more sickness and crying in the night, long after I had been given a cup of warm milk and sent off to bed.

The next morning, Mean Megan's parents came by to pick her up. The four parents sat in the kitchen for a long time, talking, and then there was yelling, briefly, between Dad and Mean Megan's dad. Then Mean Megan's family went slamming out of the house. From my bedroom window I saw them pile into their car, looking furious, and drive away.

And that had been the last of Mean Megan, and the beginning of Dexter's torment. She was not allowed out of the house, not allowed to watch TV or videos, not even allowed to go to her ballet classes, and certainly not allowed to spend the holidays at Mean Megan's house, as she had last year. It was impossible to take any pleasure in Dexter's misery, though, because Mom and Dad seemed as miserable as she did, hurt and disappointed, like those cartoon characters with little black scribbly clouds hanging over their heads. Dad even talked about canceling our holidays that summer, but Mom said we all needed some cheering up and it wasn't fair to punish everyone because of Dexter. Then she said that I would be terribly disappointed if we didn't go. Which was interesting, I thought. I wasn't supposed to have heard this conversation but happened to be playing spelunker behind the sofa when it began and didn't come out fast enough to show I was eavesdropping by accident instead of on purpose. Interesting because, though I hadn't realized it, I *would* have been terribly disappointed, and it was clever of Mom to know something about me that I didn't know myself. After a while they went away and I could come out from behind the sofa without them ever knowing I had been there.

That evening at supper, Mom and Dad began to talk about our two weeks' vacation and where we should go. This, too, was mightily interesting, since I knew they had already decided. "The lake?" I said tentatively, because this felt a bit like cheating on a test.

"That's a good idea," Dad said, as though it hadn't occurred to him. "We had a good time last year, didn't we?"

"Would you like to see the lake, Dexter?" Mom said.

"Why are you even asking me?" Dexter said. "Why are you even pretending you care what I think?" and then she started to cry again.

Mom put her arm around Dexter's shoulders and Dexter cuddled against her, crying harder. "Dexter will come to the lake," Mom said. "We'll all have a good time together and get past all this."

"We can go fishing," I said, and Dad gave me a thumbs-up, but it was hard to know if Dexter heard, because she had her face mashed into Mom's shoulder.

Things didn't really get any better, though: Dexter was still not allowed any of her privileges, and she still acted as though this was all my fault. This mostly took the form of ignoring me, walking out of the room when I spoke to her and refusing to play games with me. I played a lot of Junior Scrabble against myself. In the car, Dex declared she didn't want to go to the lake after all, and there was an argument about that. Now, as we pull into the parking lot, she's pretending to be asleep so she can be grumpy when she's "woken" and made to get out of the car. So she misses the first moments back at the lake, the first moments when it seems like we've time-traveled because everything is the same as it was last year: the damp, the fog, the quiet, even the keening bird. Now that I'm a year older, the bird sounds less frightening than sadly familiar, the expression of a mood it seems our family has been living with since Grandpa's death. I feel older. When Dad comes around to my side of the car, I tell him I feel one hundred years old.

"Me too," he says. He hugs me and together we look at the smoke-colored lake while Mom wakes Dex as gently as she can. Tonight we stay in our cabin while the smoky fog licks and creeps through the trees and along the edges of things. We eat the soup I heat on the stove, and afterward we play cards, not talking much. When it's time for bed, Mom says, "You girls sleep in tomorrow. You both look like you could use it," and I realize I'm exhausted, as though I've been awake for as long as I've been alive.

The next morning I take Dexter down to the office to show her where to get a boat key. The old man behind the counter says he remembers me even though I'm taller than last summer. Down at the jetty, I show Dexter how to unhook our pedal boat. She still isn't talking much, but she watches everything I show her and doesn't tell me to shut up. We're just climbing into our boat when a voice calls, "Don't forget your pee-eff-dee!"

I turn around. Jogging down the slope to the shore is a boy about Dexter's age, tall and slim and tanned, both familiar and unfamiliar at the same time. It takes me a second before I call back, "Robert!"

He lands lightly on the jetty and jogs over to us, grinning broadly.

"You're not fat!" I say.

Dexter buries her face in her hands.

"No, it's okay," Robert says. "It was that stupid Weight Watchers my mom made me go to. I guess it worked."

"Is your mom here too?"

Robert nods. "Just the two of us this year." I see he's happy about that. "Want to go fishing?"

Dexter pokes me in the arm.

"This is my sister, Dexter," I say, and Robert says hi and Dexter says hi in the soft shy voice she uses for boys she likes the look of. She's gone a little pink in her cheeks also. I look at Robert and roll my eyes, and he crosses his eyes at me, and I know he'll be my friend for one more summer at least.

"Let's go fishing," he says again. "The rowboat will fit all three of us."

"I don't know how to fish," Dexter says in that same bashful, appealing voice and blinks a few times for good measure. I've seen it all before.

"Well," Robert says slowly. "There's a lot to learn. But we could use a second mate."

He holds his hand out for Dexter to take and pulls her out of the boat. Maybe I made a mistake a moment before, and my summer is going to be rather lonely after all. I scramble out on my own.

"The first thing you have to do is go back up to the office and ask for some bait," he says, and when he turns back to help tie the pedal boat up again, he gives me an enormous, unmistakable wink.

That night, our parents go to bed early, leaving us flopped out in the cedar chairs on the front deck with a big bowl of popcorn and instructions to keep it down. I flip through Dexter's teen magazines while she reads one of my mystery stories. Lights from the other cabins wink through the trees, and after a while I pull my beach towel from where it was drying on the railing and drape it over my knees against the mild summer-night cool. Dexter does the same. Dexter's towel has a Hawaiian pattern on it, big bloomy flowers, blue on blue, and mine is green on green. These are new, a surprise gift from Mom when we came up from the lake this afternoon, panting and laughing and dripping and swatting at each other, Dexter saying, "I can't believe you guys did that to me!" and me saying, "I can't believe you fell for it!"

I immediately wrapped my towel around myself like a cape, but Dexter showed me how to knot it at my hip over my bathing suit, like a sarong, and we sashayed around the cabin that way for the rest of the afternoon.

"That boy has made you girls giddy," Dad said. He had spent the afternoon in a deck chair on the carpet of fragrant pine needles a little way from the cabin, turning the pages of his newspaper and humming tunelessly, like a motor.

"Daddy!" we both shrieked and collapsed laughing on the sofa, though we couldn't have said exactly why.

"When you see Robert tomorrow, invite him and his mom for dessert," Mom said. "I'll make a pumpkin pie."

"In the summer?" I said wonderingly, even though pumpkin pie is our family's favorite.

"Sure," Mom said. "We'll celebrate."

"Celebrate what?" Dexter said.

Mom and I looked at each other, and I thought, *I know what*, though I wouldn't have wanted to say it aloud. It was that we still had the whole summer ahead of us, and our whole family was happy at the same time, and that was rare enough these days to be cause for a celebration.

"Go to bed, Edie," Dexter says now, and I realize my eyes have closed and I've been drifting. "I'm coming in a minute."

Don't tell me what to do, I think. But because the night is so peaceful, the lake quietly lapping and the night bird calling every few minutes, and because we've spent such an unexpectedly pleasant day, and because I really do want to go to bed, I content myself with dropping my new towel on my sister's head as I pass by on my way back into the cabin. Smiling at Dex's thrashing limbs and muffled threats, I look forward to my sister's fierce, sweet, inevitable revenge. Maybe not tonight or tomorrow, but soon, I know. Soon.

Annabel Lyon is the author of two books of adult fiction, *Oxygen* and *The Best Thing for You*. *All-Season Edie* is her first work for children. She lives in New Westminster, British Columbia, with her husband and two children.